Vows at Dusk

A Reunion

Book Seven of The Gifted Series

Ana Ban

FIVE POINT PUBLISHING

All Persons Fictitious Disclaimer:

This book is a work of fiction. Any similarity between the characters and situations within its pages and places or persons, living or dead, is unintentional and coincidental.

ISBN 978-1-959716-19-8 (Paperback)

[1.Fantasy 2.Romance 3.Paranormal]

First Edition

Printed in the USA

Contents

Chapter 1 1

Chapter 2 10

Chapter 3 19

Chapter 4 33

Chapter 5 43

Chapter 6 51

Chapter 7 61

Chapter 8 72

Chapter 9 81

Chapter 10 91

Chapter 11 97

Chapter 12 106

Chapter 13 118

Chapter 14 128

Chapter 15 137

Chapter 16 151

Chapter 17 162

Chapter 18 174

Chapter 19 183

Chapter 20 192

After Dusk 202

Chapter 1 203

Chapter 2 214

Chapter 3 222

Chapter 4 232

Chapter 5 240

Chapter 6 249

Chapter 7 261

Chapter 8 271

Chapter 9 278

Chapter 10 288
Chapter 11 294
Chapter 12 302
Chapter 13 309
Other books by Ana Ban 316

For a full family tree, please visit
www.anabannovels.com/gifted-tree

Chapter 1

Standing on the balcony off her bedroom, Jade took in the breathtaking sight before her as the sun slowly rose over the burst of autumn color that painted the woods in hues of crimson, gold, and orange. A small, contented smile hovered on her lips, seemingly etched there permanently by the sheer joy and peace that filled her heart. The crisp morning air carried with it the earthy scent of fallen leaves and the promise of a new day, and Jade inhaled deeply, savoring the tranquility of the early hour. One hand gripped the smooth, wooden rail, anchoring her to the present moment, while the other rested against her stomach.

Nerves had arrived along with the first of the guests and as the final preparations for the wedding had begun. Nerves that were born not of her decision to finally tie the knot but by being the center of attention to hundreds of people. That included her own enormous bunch, Talon's newfound extended family, and the hordes of Elementals they'd invited to their small town in Northern Wisconsin.

Talon joined her in his silent way, arms sliding around her middle and his chin coming to rest against her shoulder. Jade sighed happily, memorizing everything about this moment. "Your mom and sisters will be here soon."

Turning in his arms, Jade rested her palms against his chest. "I love you, you know."

"As I love you." His widening smile took her breath away. Their lips met, and she crushed her body to his, always eager for intimacy. With a chuckle, he pulled away, gripping her upper arms with a tender yet unbreakable hold. "Your family will be here soon; we cannot."

Rolling her eyes, Jade pouted. "You're no fun."

Leaning in, he pressed his lips against the base of her neck, his breath hot against her skin and shooting sparks along her veins. "I'll make it up to you, I promise."

Jade could swear her knees turned to liquid. Resting her head against his chest, she closed her eyes and took a deep breath of the scent that was wholly Talon: campfires and evergreens. They both could hear the sound of tires along the dirt drive, and she relented with a soft sigh.

"Later," Jade said sternly, making her point with her finger. Shaking her wrist at him like one would while scolding a child, she added, "Or else."

"Anything for you, love." Talon disappeared down the stairs to welcome their guests, leaving Jade to dress on her own.

She sighed; her news would have to wait.

"Final fitting!" Pearl's voice drifted easily up the stairs. Though Jade felt ready for the onslaught, dressed in a slip with a robe tied over the top, her pulse picked up with anxiety as her mom, Madeline, along with her three sisters—Amber, Emma, and Pearl—bustled into the room, excitement tangible in the air.

Pearl had an overstuffed garment bag draped over her arm. With a deep breath, Jade pasted a smile on her face and braced for a long morning. It wasn't that she wasn't excited. It was more that Jade had let her family plan out this huge affair when she would have been perfectly happy running off to Vegas with Talon. In fact, in her mind, they were already married in the way of his people. Mates—soulmates, if you will—were much more permanent than a human marriage.

But the smiles on her family's faces were worth all the trouble. Emma and Pearl pulled her into the large bathroom and helped her into the soft white satin. Emma and Rick were recently engaged but had decided to wait until the next summer for their wedding. After everything Talon and Jade had been through over the past several months, they'd decided that they had waited long enough.

It also gave them a good excuse to invite all the Elementals they could find in order to meet and plan. Something had to be done about the daemons. With Samhain just weeks away, they had to put together a team to travel to Ireland and find the entrance to Mag Mell. The otherworld.

As the dress fell against the floor with a *whoosh*, Jade looked at herself in the mirror. She still couldn't believe how perfect it was. The bodice had a sweetheart neckline and elbow-length sleeves, while the full skirt gathered together at uneven intervals, giving it a little style. Across the waist, a strip of white leather with a beaded turquoise design hugged her midsection as a way to bring Talon's culture together with her own.

Madeline came in with tears in her eyes. "Oh, you look so beautiful."

"Thanks, Mom," Jade said, turning to her with eyes damper than usual. "I love it."

A knock on the outer door announced the arrival of Lani and Raven. Jade had asked Lani to be her maid of honor, while Raven had thrown herself into helping with wedding preparations. Jade liked the girl's spunk.

Over the past months, Jade found she really liked all of Samson's—and Talon's—family. It filled her heart to see Lani not only with her mate but with her own family as well. Raven held up a gift bag and grinned. "We brought you something! And we kicked Talon out, so he can't peek."

Curious as to what they were up to, Jade accepted the bag and looked inside. Before she could decipher the jumble of material, Raven took over, bringing out the headpiece with a flourish. "Since you didn't want a veil, anyway, we thought we'd make you this. Lani, Nova, Tala, Valentina, Lenna, and I all helped."

"I mostly watched," Lani corrected.

"It's beautiful," Jade said on a breath, feeling tears spring forth again. "And perfect. Thank you so much."

Amber took it carefully from Raven and placed it on the bride's head. Though her hair would be styled, it completed the outfit perfectly. All the women in the room breathed out a sigh simultaneously, and Jade broke the serene moment by bursting out in laughter.

"What?" Pearl asked, startled.

"You all just sighed completely in sync," Jade said, another bubble of laughter escaping.

As they glanced at each other, they all began to chuckle. It seemed more forced than necessary, as if they were placating her. Pearl frowned. "Leave it to you to ruin a beautiful moment."

"Laughter is good for the soul," Jade said. "But seriously, thank you all so much. I couldn't have done any of this without you."

"Oh, we know," Emma said. "You'd have eloped to Vegas wearing blue jeans."

This time, everyone else laughed but Jade. She couldn't even deny the claim—she'd been thinking that same thing just a few minutes earlier. "All right, get me out of this thing before I spill something on it."

Amber removed the headpiece first, then stepped back as Pearl and Emma helped her out of the dress. The rest of the ladies made their way downstairs while Jade disappeared into the closet to dress. Pulling on jeans and a comfortable shirt, she came back out to find Pearl zipping the garment bag.

"I'll take these with me since you'll be staying at my house."

It was a silly tradition, but one in which her sisters had convinced her to participate. Thinking about spending even one night away from Talon already gave her palpitations. Nodding, Jade followed Pearl down the stairs to join the rest of the group. Madeline had spread out all kinds of books across the large dining table—everything from seating charts to photos of flower arrangements. Jade looked over her mom's shoulder and stifled a grimace. "Anything I can help with?"

"Oh, don't be silly," she said, fluttering her hand to shoo Jade away. Raven sat at Madeline's right hand, as she had been since arriving.

Shrugging, Jade ventured into the kitchen to make coffee and tea for everyone. It was the only thing she was allowed to do.

Lani stepped away from the bustle of women and joined her side. "Reya and Tristan arrived late last night."

"Oh, I can't wait to see the twins," Jade said with a grin. "They've probably grown so much since the summer."

"It's only been a couple of months," Lani said, but couldn't hide the joy on her face at having found her family. "Samson and I will be going to New Zealand after Ireland. I can't wait to see my home again."

"You're set on helping the daemons?"

"Yes. I owe it to them. They came with to meet with the Elementals, but they don't feel comfortable coming to the wedding."

"Why not?"

Lani raised her eyebrows. "Your wedding is on the full moon."

Right. Jade knew that. "Sorry. Wedding stress. Couldn't we do a spell or something? So that any humans wouldn't see the horns?"

"That's not a bad idea. I'll speak with Frances."

"I'm sure Frances would love to help. Lani, I'm so happy for you. Samson, your family...." Jade told her not for the first time, resting a palm against Lani's wrist. "Are you and Samson going to have a wedding ceremony?"

"Perhaps something small on the reservation. I'm sure his family would like that. Raven certainly would."

"She's definitely got a future in wedding planning if she wants it."

"When are the rest of the Elementals arriving?"

"Should be now," Jade said, checking the time. "Talon's helping to get them all settled." *Has everyone arrived?* she asked across their telepathic link.

Just about. I've finished showing the former shadowmen from the compound to where they'll be staying. Reya and Tristan are at the bed-and-breakfast, along with Aden. Kate is on her way to you now while Hugh and Jared help me get everyone else settled. Reese and Dominic, along with Dominic's brother and mate, should be arriving soon.

When Jade had last talked to Reese, she'd explained about Emerson's mate, Arie. A shadowman had converted Arie, and her soul—along with her blood—suffered the effects. Reese hoped that Reya, Kate, and Jade would be able to help her.

That's great. I'll come as soon as I'm able.

No rush, love. You ladies enjoy yourselves.

Turning back to Lani, Jade relayed what Talon had said while she prepped a tray with the finished drinks. They both moved back to the dining room as Jade set the tray on the table. "Kate's on her way."

As she spoke, a knock sounded on the door. Lani answered and ushered Kate inside. Jade was the first to embrace her cousin, but Kate quickly got engulfed in hugs by the rest of the group.

"What can I do to help?" Kate asked and, unlike Jade, was immediately given a task.

Jade hovered, refilling glasses as needed and offering an assortment of snacks. It only made her feel useless. After an hour, Jade exchanged glances with Kate and Lani. Not only was she going stir-crazy, Jade knew they were needed elsewhere.

"Would we be all right to leave?" she asked her mom. "I wanted to go say hi to some of our guests."

"Sure, sweetie. We'll just stay here and wrap up."

Worked for her. Kissing Madeline on the cheek, Jade waved to her sisters and led Lani and Kate out. They took a car, though running would have been faster. Jade's family remained blissfully ignorant to the existence of Elementals or anything supernatural. For now, that was how it had to stay.

Kate drove, wanting to keep her car at the bed-and-breakfast where she and Hugh would be staying. Jade and Kate would catch up with Reya, and then the three of them would see what, if anything, they could do for Arie.

After that, Jade needed to speak privately with Reya herself.

Chapter 2

Snuggling against Tristan's chest, Reya savored the last few minutes of quiet before daybreak. Leia and Nicola slept peacefully in the next room, but they woke like clockwork every morning. Stroking a hand against his chest, Reya let out a contented sigh. "I can't remember the last time I felt this relaxed."

His arm tightened around her waist, and she could feel his desire against her thigh. The chemistry between them hadn't dimmed; if anything, it had grown. Thank goodness the children slept at night, and they didn't. "Perhaps I could help you feel more relaxed." Tristan's deep, husky voice sent waves of warmth rushing over her.

"You're insatiable," Reya said with a light laugh, having no quarrel with that.

"We are still technically newlyweds. We have no battles to fight, and our family is whole. What else is there to do?"

"What else, indeed?" Reya smirked, but any further thought quickly cut off when his lips met hers. The fire consumed them as they moved together in perfect harmony. His hands caressed down her back, gripping against her waist and pulling her fully against his chest. With his eyes holding hers captive, Tristan joined them together on a sigh.

They fit together like two puzzle pieces—each made perfectly for the other. His mouth seized control of hers as he took the lead, building the need in Reya until she felt like she would implode. Her core tightened and spasmed, forcing her to draw her head back to gulp in air.

Tristan. She called his name silently, begging for the release only he could give.

Stay with me, tau o te ate.

"I can't. It's too much."

"Reya." He said her name softly. "Look at me."

Their eyes locked together. The love that passed between them seemed nearly tangible, beautiful ribbons of color flowing between and around their entwined bodies. Reya hovered on the brink of release but did as he asked, holding on just a little while longer. His mouth crushed hers as their world spun out, her limbs shaking with the force of it.

Tristan's arms remained in a vice grip around her waist as their hearts slowed. Reya rested her head in the crook of his neck, perfectly content to use him as her pillow.

"We should get up," he said, though he clearly had no intention of moving.

"Mm," she murmured in response.

"How about a shower before the twins wake?" he asked, and she detected a wicked note in his voice.

Before Reya could respond, he stood with her still in his arms, their bodies still locked together. In the next moment, they were under a stream of cool water, which quickly warmed to hot. Not that she noticed. Steam rose from her skin as Tristan's mouth once again found hers, traveling down her neck and across her chest. He already moved inside her, pushing her forever toward that brink.

Feed, tau o te ate. You will need your strength.

He didn't have to ask twice. Her incisors lengthened, and as the first spicy mixture of Tristan's blood hit her tongue, Reya's body responded in the only way it knew how.

She spiraled out of control, thankful for Tristan's strong grip as she was sure her legs were useless. Drinking her fill, Reya closed the wound as she felt the cool tile against her back. They were both careening toward the cliff with no chance of slowing. His name was on her lips as they flew off the edge and into the stars, light exploding behind her lids as she clung to him for dear life.

For several minutes they sucked in deep breaths until Tristan finally placed Reya back on her feet. They held her weight with shaky strength, so she continued to grip Tristan's biceps for balance. "What will you do while I examine Emerson's mate?"

Reya had spoken with Reese a few weeks ago and had planned to meet with Arie when she arrived. Though Reese hadn't gone into detail on what the woman had been through, only that she would be more comfortable with a female healer, Reya knew Arie was in bad shape, possibly needing help from Kate and Jade as well.

"Jared, Hugh, and Kate are arriving with the former shadowmen this morning," Tristan replied, spreading soap across Reya's skin. "I would like to see them."

"I've missed Jared." They'd grown close when Reya first arrived in New Zealand and Tristan had been subdued by the effects of a drug aimed specifically toward Elementals. Plus, Jared was technically family. "Hugh and Kate, too, of course."

"It will be interesting to see how the former shadowmen have fared, as well. Jared told me they have all found work."

"That's great news," Reya said. Just the fact alone that Kate and Jade had been able to heal so many formerly evil creatures was incredible. Before she could say anything further, they heard the tiny voices that immediately filled her heart with joy.

"I'll get them," Tristan said, placing another kiss against her neck. "You finish."

Enjoying the view as Tristan stepped out, Reya washed her hair and dressed so she could join her mate and children. Tristan had already gotten them dressed, and the three were playing on the floor when she exited the bathroom.

"Mama!" Though only six months old, the twins were developing at the Elemental rate and were not only speaking—though not full sentences—but both had also taken their first steps. Nicola pushed himself to his hands and feet, his butt sticking up in the air until he straightened and took a few wobbly steps forward. Leia crawled her way to Reya and beat her brother by seconds.

Gathering them in her arms, Reya buried her face against their hair and inhaled their scents. "Hi, babies."

There was a soft knock at the door which Tristan answered. Aden waited on the other side, brightening on seeing Leia. In response, she wiggled out of Reya's arms and crawled toward him. Aden met her halfway and scooped her up. "Morning, Aden. How was your night?"

"Good. I familiarized myself with the area. It's a beautiful part of the country."

"Can't argue there," Reya agreed, kissing Tristan. "Have fun with the boys."

"And you reach out to me immediately if you need assistance."

"I promise."

If it is too dangerous, we will figure out another plan of action.

You worry too much.

You are my life, tau o te ate. I will do anything to keep you from harm.

I love you, too. Stealing one more kiss, Reya winked for reassurance and stepped into the hall.

Both kids were squirming with energy, so Aden set Leia down while Nicola tightened a fist in Reya's pant leg for balance. Aden glanced over at Reya with a concerned frown. "Could this be dangerous for you?"

Rolling her eyes, Reya let out a sigh. It was one thing for Tristan to worry, quite another for Aden. "I'm a doctor. I deal with these situations all the time."

"Forgive me for saying so, but healing broken bones or treating human disease is vastly different from dealing with an unknown Elemental."

"It's still my job, Aden. I'll do everything in my power to help her." To change the subject, Reya sent him a half-smile and gestured ahead where Leia was about to disappear around a corner of the hallway. "You're sure you can handle them?"

"Of course, no prob—no! Leia, you must be careful!" Aden loped over to Reya's daughter in a split second, rescuing her from the impending doom of the staircase.

The little girl with eyes so like her fathers placed a hand against Aden's cheek. In a tiny voice, she asked, "Outside?"

"Of course," Aden said. "After we find your brother. Where did Nicola go?"

Panic-stricken eyes met Reya's, and she allowed another bubble of laughter to surface. Here she'd thought Tristan would be the overprotective one with the children, but Aden had him beat. Twisting around, Reya nudged Nicola from behind her legs with a gentle hand. "Go with Aden."

With a devilish grin, Nicola raised his arms, the universal gesture for 'up.' Obliging him, Reya scooped him into her arms and planted kisses over his adorable face.

"I hope I'm not long," Reya said, following Aden down the stairs of the lovely bed-and-breakfast. "But in case I am, you're sure you don't mind watching the kids?"

"Of course not. Have you talked more to Reese, found out what, exactly, is wrong?" Now that he'd expressed his concern for Reya, she could see how hearing about another woman in pain had him worried. He had a soft spot for women in danger.

"No. Reese didn't want to get into it over the phone. Jace offered to help when he was with them in Europe, but it didn't work out. Reese thought she would be more comfortable with a woman."

"Makes sense," Aden said, nodding thoughtfully.

"Kate and Jade are going to meet with us, too," Reya added, thankful to have the talented women assist with this delicate matter.

As they reached the front doors, Leia immediately began wiggling, eager to be in touch with the earth. She had a natural affinity for it, an ability that grew daily. Aden set her carefully on her feet, where she immediately took off for the thick grass.

Allowing Nicola to join her, Reya made a sweep of the guests. It had been a wonderful idea for Jade to invite all the Elementals she could find to her wedding. Now that Jared had been reunited with Hugh, and Tristan had found his sister, Reya's little family had grown exponentially.

Down the path, she spotted Reese with her mate, Dominic. They'd met by chance and had been lucky to. Not only had she led Reya, Tristan, and Jared back to Hugh, her keen wit was a welcome addition to the group.

Directly behind Dominic walked a man obviously his twin. Emerson had the same sparkling green eyes and dark, side-swept hair as his brother. Next to him, a beautiful woman with haunted eyes watched the scene nervously. Reya recognized her hesitance for what it was.

She had been through terrible, terrible things, and her firm grip on Emerson's hand was the only thing anchoring her. Reya had a feeling that without his presence, she'd bolt.

As they approached, Aden chased after the twins who had wandered a bit too far for his liking. Reya smiled welcomingly to the group, though her senses expanded to find out as much as she could about her patient. Arie had stunning, long blonde hair and baby blue eyes.

The shade and shape of which were oddly familiar...

Arie turned to the side, checking her peripherals while speaking to her mate, and the cut of her jaw was as familiar to Reya as her own. Heart beating with unrivaled excitement, knowing he could hear her even across this distance, Reya spoke softly. "Aden."

As soon as she said his name, even though the approaching group was still a hundred feet away, Arie's eyes snapped to Reya's. Aden jogged forward at Reya's call, glancing over at the newcomers out of habit.

Aden and Arie's eyes locked, recognition flickering in their depths.

The breath knocked from his lungs, Aden barely managed a word. A name. "Aurelia."

Chapter 3

Arie's hand gripped Emerson's so tightly it was lucky he was a supernatural creature with supernatural strength. Otherwise, it may have been broken.

He looked down with a private smile, the kind that made her feel like the only woman in the world. When Arie attempted to return the gesture, it felt full of trepidation. She looked away again, over the wide green lawn sprinkled with colorful autumn leaves. The air had a crispness to it that felt refreshing instead of cold. The ones getting married—whom she was about to meet—had certainly chosen their date wisely.

It will be all right, Emerson assured her again.

She hated that she needed the constant reminder. *I'm not afraid.*

You are the strongest, bravest woman I have ever met. Their eyes met, the spark of love and longing plain for anyone to see.

What if they can't help me? It was that question, along with the repercussions of it, that had Arie squeezing his hand so tight.

I'll never be accepted into their world the way I am. Which means they won't accept you. Or Edith, or Anya.

Though the two women Arie considered sisters had traveled to Wisconsin, they chose to remain away from the festivities. Had it been strictly up to Anya, Arie believed they would be there now—but Edith wasn't ready for such a large group of people, and Anya decided to stay with her.

After Arie met with Reya, Jade, and Kate, if what they tried worked, she hoped the three women could help Edith and Anya as well—just not around all these other Elementals.

These are good people, according to Dominic. And if the worst case happens, then we will leave and never look back. We have each other, my brother and Reese, Edith and Anya—not to mention Jace. That is all we need.

Jace. He was connected to these people. Had grown up with several of them. They wouldn't turn out his mate, too, would they? That is, if Edith ever accepted their connection. Taking a deep breath, Arie nodded and looked forward again. There were a lot of Elementals in the large yard surrounding the bed-and-breakfast, all with bright, smiling faces. Dominic and Reese led the way, looking for Reya. Reese had also asked Jade and Kate to come, who had apparently helped other shadowmen heal their souls. While the concept interested Arie, she knew it would be strange to meet shadowmen that she wasn't trying to kill.

In front of the group stood a beautiful woman whose dark hair had red streaks shining brightly in the sun. Her strange amber eyes, glowing with intelligence, had settled on Arie. Suddenly feeling anxious again, Arie tilted her head to look up at Emerson. *You'll stay with me the whole time, right?*

Of course.

"Aden."

Arie's head snapped up automatically at the name. Her brother's name. Even after all these years, his loss still left a hole in her heart. The name had been uttered by the woman with the amber eyes, and she stared at Arie in shock. As a man ran toward Reya, Arie's gaze switched to his, and everything inside her stilled.

Aden.

Her brother.

How could this be?

Aden was dead. She'd watched him die. Was this some cruel trick? Had these people already decided she wasn't worth saving and were taunting her?

"Aurelia," the man said on barely a breath.

He'd said her name. Her real name. Arie had only ever told it to Emerson, and he wouldn't have betrayed her like that.

"Arie? What's going on?" Reese asked, as they'd all paused as a group.

Do you know this man? Emerson asked privately as he subtly shifted to stand protectively in front of his mate.

"It's...it's my brother," Arie finally admitted, tears springing to her eyes.

In an instant, Aden was running, gripping Arie by her shoulders as he searched her face. When he finally managed words, his voice broke. "Is it really you?"

"How can this be?" Arie said simultaneously.

They stared at each other for several beats of time until Aden gave in and wrapped his arms around his sister. Her next words were muffled against his chest. "I saw you die."

"You were taken," he answered. "I thought I'd lost you."

"I thought I'd lost *you.*"

They broke their embrace, though he only took half a step back. Dimly aware of the crowd surrounding them, Arie felt the first tear leak down her cheek. His own eyes filled. "It's really you."

Her throat clogged with tears, Arie merely nodded. She felt a gentle hand against her back and accepted the offered handkerchief. Using it to swipe at the escaped tears, she introduced her brother to her mate. "Aden, this is Emerson. My...boyfriend."

She hesitated in the introduction, realizing she didn't know how much Aden knew about Elementals. She took another moment to analyze her brother, realizing she felt a connection more than just siblings. He wasn't just Gifted, though. He had been converted. They had much to discuss.

Aden grinned at Emerson, offering his hand and speaking the words on Arie's mind. "It seems we have quite a bit to catch up on."

"Arie? I'm Reya," said the woman who waited just behind Aden, holding a little girl in her arms. A small boy clung to her leg, grinning mischievously up at Arie. "I'm the healer."

Aden's concerned gaze turned back to his sister. "What is going on?"

Letting out a breath, Arie clasped Emerson's hand again. He was her rock, her anchor. "It's a long story. Is there somewhere more private we can go?"

An intimidating, dark-featured man appeared beside Reya. Arie could see the resemblance in the eyes to the small children, but his countenance instantly put her on guard. "Aurelia, welcome. I am Tristan, Reya's mate. Aden has been searching for you for a long time. And you must be Emerson," he added, extending his hand to shake Emerson's. "Nice to meet you, as well. Please feel free to use our suite of rooms. I will send Kate and Jade up once they arrive."

Reese looked over at Arie. "Do you want us to come with?"

A silent exchange happened between the brothers. Dominic answered before Arie could. "Why don't Reese and I watch the twins so Arie and her brother can catch up?"

Reese's eyes lit up. "Oh, we'd be happy to." Kneeling, she held out her hands for Nicola. "What do you say? Want to hang out with me and this big teddy bear?"

Nicola looked up at his mom then back to Reese. With his adorable smile, he held his hands out to Reese and allowed her to pick him up. Leia studied Dominic with wisdom that belied her infant age before reaching out. Arie couldn't tell who was more surprised by the easy acquiescence—Reya, Dominic, or her own brother.

"Call for us if you need anything," Dominic said to Emerson and Arie. "We'll be close."

"They've just fed, so you shouldn't have any issues. Here is the bag with anything you could possibly need," Reya said to Reese, taking the diaper bag from Aden and handing it over. "We're in room two-oh-five if you need us."

After kissing her babies on the forehead, Reya linked hands with Tristan and led Aden, Emerson, and Arie into the bed-and-breakfast.

They trudged silently up the stairs, words unnecessary for the moment. Arie still had a hard time believing what she saw was real. Aden must have felt the same, for he kept glancing back at her as if checking she hadn't disappeared. *This isn't a trick, right?*

No, I don't believe so. I'm so happy for you.

She could feel the warmth of Emerson's love through their link, and she reveled in its light. *Whatever happens next, I love you.*

Her eyes met his, and she felt instantly lost in the glittering green depth. *You are my life,* he replied simply.

Reya opened their door and allowed their guests to enter first. There were two connecting rooms with a bath between them. Aden pulled out seats from the small kitchen table and offered them to Emerson and Arie. She sat with Emerson beside her while Aden perched opposite.

"We will wait for Jade and Kate downstairs and bring them up when they arrive," Tristan said, Reya smiling in agreement. It was their way of allowing Aden and Arie time together to reacquaint, which Arie greatly appreciated.

Once the couple left, Aden told his sister of his life since she'd last seen him: waking to men who brought him into a torture camp; meeting Reya, when she'd been brought in; helping her rescue Tristan and escape. Almost dying, again, and converting into an Elemental to be saved. The year since working to shut down the camps that Donovan had spearheaded.

"Please, tell me about you. What's going on that you need three healers?"

As he asked, a knock sounded on the door. Two women who were obviously related stepped in while Reya held the door open.

Jade had a petite stature, with straight blonde hair and green eyes, while her cousin, Kate, was closer to Arie's height and had fiery red hair with the same green eyes as Jade.

"No way, you're Aden's sister?" Jade exclaimed immediately. "That's so awesome. I'm so happy you two found each other!"

"That is incredible," Kate agreed with a smile. "I guess this reunion Jade forced on us was a good idea, after all."

"All my ideas are good," said the smaller woman with an indignant look. Arie envied their easy banter. "So, tell us about you, about why we're here."

With a deep breath, Arie squeezed Emerson's hand and decided not to beat around the bush. "The shadowman who captured me also converted me. My blood is tainted, as is my soul." She said this starkly, not expecting sympathy. She didn't want sympathy. "When Emerson and I first met, we connected through the earth. Our souls were laid bare, and we could both see mine is darkened. Shadowed. I haven't allowed him to drink my blood, though the need is there as mates."

"I'm so sorry for all you've been through," Jade said immediately, placing her hand against Arie's arm. A strange tingling sensation ran along Arie's skin, and oddly, she felt her spirits rise and the constant pain lessen.

Arie's eyes shot to hers as she realized this was part of Jade's gift. Hers tightened with strain for a moment before clearing. "You took on some of my pain, didn't you?"

Jade nodded, her teeth gritted. "It's how my gift works."

"Don't do it, then. I wouldn't wish this on anyone."

Easing into a smile, Jade tried to be reassuring. "Don't worry. It's what I do."

"Reya? How do you think we should begin?" Kate asked.

"I would like to examine her first," Reya said decisively. "You didn't come across tainted blood in the shadowmen you rescued, correct?"

"No," Kate answered. "Just their darkened souls."

"Then I would like to start there. Arie? Or do you prefer Aurelia? Is that all right with you?"

Shrugging, Arie tried to look nonchalant. "I go by Arie now, but Aurelia is fine. You do whatever you think is best."

"Why don't you lay down on the bed?" Reya suggested. "Emerson can stay beside you."

Nodding, Arie stood and walked the short distance to the bed. Emerson stood beside her, his hand still firmly around hers while Reya pulled a chair closer. Aden sat on the opposite side, taking up her free hand and giving it a squeeze.

Kate and Jade stood at the end of the bed, watching. Arie felt like a specimen in an experiment.

Just look at me. No one else is here, Emerson said into her mind. His eyes softened when she gazed up at him. *We will fix this. I am here with you.*

Keeping her gaze steady on his, she felt a peculiar warmth spreading throughout her body. From what Jace had explained to her when he'd tried this, healers detached themselves from their body and sent their spirit seeking into another. Thinking about it too much kind of creeped her out, so Arie breathed steadily and kept her focus on her mate instead.

After several minutes, Reya blinked the room back into focus, and Arie finally looked to her. "How bad is it?"

"Nothing we can't fix," she said with a gentle smile. She then looked over to Jade and Kate, who stood at the ready. "I think we should try this simultaneously."

For a long moment, silence descended upon the room. Kate's eyebrows knit together. "We've never done anything like that before."

"You're nervous about something," Jade added, studying Reya's expression. "What is it?"

Reya looked at Arie before answering. "The shadow has been attacking your system for many years. It won't go easily. I'm afraid if I eradicate it from your blood, it will only grow stronger in your mind and soul. Our best chance is to attack it head-on, at the same time. It will be weaker fighting all three of us at once.”

Arie swallowed hard and focused first on Aden, then on Emerson. Her lifeline. *This sounds dangerous.*

It is your decision. I will support whatever you decide.

Sighing, she thought about life without pain. About Edith and Anya, depending on her to be strong. She nodded at the three women. “Do it.”

“Okay. Emerson, as soon as I give you the signal, I want you to give Arie your blood. Jade, Kate, have your mates on standby to replenish yours. Tristan is here for me, and Aden?”

“I will give as needed.”

“Okay. Ready?” Jade and Kate nodded, though they remained where they were. Arie trembled with nerves, but the men by her side kept her steady. Reya took a deep breath. “Now.”

This time, Arie watched as her expression turned blank, and immediately felt Reya’s warmth invading her system. Simultaneously, she watched as Kate’s aura began to glow, bright white with the strangest mix of colors undulating along the outside.

Her own aura revealed itself, though no one else in the room had changed. The darkness made her sick, and as Kate began to coax it away, she felt Jade moving through her mind. The part of Arie that was wholly Arie felt the soothing presence and welcomed it; the shadowed part, however, treated Jade as an intruder and tried to throw her out.

Jade had a will of iron, forcing her way through and straight into Arie's memories. They delved so deep Arie opened her eyes into another world; her childhood. Eighteen-year-old Aden had just taken over guardianship. He had always been there for her, no matter what. He raised her when they had no one left. He made Arie who she was.

Time flipped forward until the day that had replayed so many times in her nightmares. The day in New Zealand, when shadowmen had captured her and hurt Aden. At least now, when they approached the segment where he collapsed to the ground and she got whisked away, a part of Arie knew he would live. It made what came next more endurable.

This time when Arie's eyes opened, they were met with darkness. Maurice's face flashed above her, his sneer making her flinch now just as it had then. His lips pulled back in a snarl. "Hello, pet. Welcome to your new home."

"I'll never stay here with you," she shouted back.

His hand reached out and slapped across her cheek, forcing tears to spring to her eyes. She cried out from the pain, weak and terrified. He beat her until she curled into a ball and gave up on life. She'd lost her parents, her brother. She had nothing left to live for, and Arie didn't want to spend another second with this horrible creature.

She welcomed death.

Even through the haze of agony, she felt a sharp prick against her throat. The sensation surprised Arie; she'd thought she was past feeling. Her head got light and woozy. She teetered on the edge of consciousness, the sweet oblivion she'd sought so close she could almost taste it. Reaching for it, welcoming it with open arms, Arie sighed with relief.

Too late, she realized she shouldn't have opened her mouth. Hot, vile liquid poured down her throat. Arie struggled against it, the thick fluid gurgling in her throat as she choked and attempted to breathe. Was she drowning? No. Death backed away as writhing pain settled in her veins, shifting her organs and taking control of her blood.

Tears flowed down her cheeks. She couldn't fight it anymore. He'd won.

"Arie," came a sweet, cleansing voice. Struggling to open her eyes, Arie searched for the face in the darkness. "Aurelia. I'm here. Stop drinking. You'll be all right. Come with me."

When she opened her mouth to respond, more of the thick liquid poured inside, cutting off all words. "You can control what happens. Stop drinking. You're safe now."

You're safe now.

The words restored her strength, her will to live. To fight. Her eyes shot open again, and this time, she could see Jade's face.

She smiled at Arie, holding her hand out for Arie to grasp. As she did, the darkness disappeared. Maurice disappeared. Her bruised and battered body felt strong and whole.

Jade stepped into a bright white light and, without looking back, Arie followed.

Chapter 4

Arie's body began shaking, violent convulsions that forced the two men beside her into action. Emerson dropped to his knees, his hands cupping her face while he murmured in her ear. Aden gripped both her shoulders in an attempt to hold her in place.

"Fight, Aurelia! I can't lose you now. Fight!" Aden yelled, his voice breaking with tears.

Kate felt helpless to do anything, as she could see everything happening but still concentrated on coaxing Arie's soul to trust hers. If Kate broke contact now, she might lose her forever. This wasn't Arie's choosing, and the wretched creature that had a hold of her wasn't letting her go without a fight. In a way, it reminded Kate of the shadowmen they'd been unable to save; those that turned to the darkness on their own and hadn't left a path back to the light.

Those creatures had been destroyed, just as the one who had turned Arie, though a piece of him lived on through her.

But not for long, if Kate could help it.

Reya and Jade were fighting their own battles while the men continued their attempt to reach Arie. Kate knew she wouldn't be able to hear them since she was trapped in her own memories with Jade—it was up to the two of them to find their way out.

Fight, Kate encouraged the brightness of her soul. It cringed back, cowering behind the darkness. *Step aside, foul beast,* Kate directed to the darkness. *You are no longer welcome here.*

It snarled and snapped at her light, and Kate stumbled back in surprise.

That was new. Incensed now, Kate straightened her shoulders and stood firm. *You will leave us now, and never return.*

The darkness snarled again, but it had no effect this time.

Stand up and fight! Kate called out to the faint light hovering there, watching intently. *You are the goodness. You can defeat this monster!*

Her soul quivered but didn't retreat. Encouraged, Kate called to her again. *Join me and be free. Live your life the way you were meant to.*

It felt like that moment of weightlessness as a plane reached its apex, moments before a tailspin slams the passengers against their seats. Like every creature held its collective breath. No movement, no noise. As if all life's balance rested on the decision of that little speck of light buried against the dark.

With a surge of power, the light swelled and swallowed the darkness, Arie's very soul reaching out and colliding with Kate's. The power of it soared out as a shockwave and Kate flew back, bracing for impact against the wall.

Two strong arms caught her, and she breathed a sigh of relief.

Hugh. *Thank you,* she exhaled into his mind, feeling exhausted for the first time since she'd begun healing shadowmen.

Anytime, he replied with a smirk.

Beside them, Talon had arrived and braced Jade as she still worked through the terrors in Arie's mind. Tristan had managed to keep Reya in an upright position. When Kate's gaze landed on Arie's still shaking form, she realized Emerson stared at her in shock. This was the first time he'd witnessed what Kate could do.

"Her soul is won," Kate assured them. "Now it's up to Jade and Reya."

Emerson nodded, his mouth tight with tension. As he began murmuring to Arie once more, Kate turned in Hugh's arms and soaked up his strength. "How did you know?"

"I was in your mind with you," he said. It seemed their connection grew stronger every day. "Talon and I were waiting outside."

"Batman to the rescue," Kate said, nuzzling into his neck.

Take what you need.

Her incisors lengthened, and she took her fill of the spicy concoction that was wholly Hugh and made specifically for her. Trying to remain conscious of the others in the room, as taking his blood tended to be a highly erotic act, Kate quickly closed the wound but took an extra moment to breathe in his scent.

That was quite the battle.

I was equal parts terrified and proud of you.

Turning her attention back to the rest of the room, Kate knew it could be some time before Jade completed her task. Arie had stopped convulsing, but Emerson had yet to move from his position. Kate could hear the raw emotion in his voice and felt for him.

Aden had released his hold on Arie's shoulders but looked to Reya with concern. She grew paler by the second. "Something's wrong."

Tristan nodded stiffly. "Get Jace. I'm going to connect to Reya and find out what's wrong."

Tristan cradled Reya like a child and murmured into her ear before his face went completely blank. Hugh disappeared from the room to find Jace, returning just a few minutes later. Kate hadn't met Jace in person; she only knew him from stories that Hugh and Jared had told her.

The man with dark hair and shock blue eyes quickly assessed the situation before looking at Emerson. Arie's mate looked strained, sweat dripping from his forehead as he lent her whatever strength he was able. Kate had never seen an Elemental sweat before. This couldn't be good.

A silent and mutual understanding passed between Emerson and Jace. At Emerson's nod, Jace shed his body and moved through Arie's. Kate prayed two healers were enough to win this battle.

They all felt a surge of power in the room. Reya twitched as the infusion from both Tristan and Jace helped to reenergize her depleted cells. The connection between mates—the potential there—continued to amaze.

Jade's eyes fluttered open next. That had been much quicker than her expeditions in the past.

Thankfully, Talon's arms were wrapped securely around her, for seconds later, her eyes rolled up into the back of her head, and she collapsed. Talon sank to the ground with Jade in his lap. "Jade! Baby, come back to me. Open your eyes for me. Jade?"

Hugh and Kate rushed to her side, a collective sigh of relief sounding when she blinked up at Talon. "What happened? Why's everyone staring at me?"

"You fainted, love," Talon said gently.

"I did not! You know perfectly well I don't faint."

Talon smirked, his relief palpable. "She always says that after she faints."

Jade rolled her eyes and got to her feet with Talon's help. During their time in California, Kate had never seen Jade faint after healing a shadowman, though she'd said it had happened the first couple of times she'd done a healing session. Kate had been physically attacked by the shadowed part of Arie's soul. Reya looked as if she was fading fast.

Whatever Maurice had done was powerful, indeed. Before Kate could pepper Jade with questions, she allowed Talon a little privacy for Jade to refuel. Tristan, Jace, and Reya were still gone to this world while the final battle ensued.

Once Jade had her fill, she explained quietly what had happened in Arie's memories. "How long was I out?"

"Less than an hour," Kate said with a shrug. "Way less time than normal."

"Hm," she murmured but didn't say anything further. Kate knew her well enough to know she had an idea why that was but wasn't willing to share at the moment.

All eyes were on Tristan and the healers, helpless to do anything but watch. The minutes ticked by in silence. No one dared move or speak. Aden had tears flowing steadily down his cheeks. Emerson's eyes were closed tight, his breathing ragged.

Finally, Tristan's eyes popped open. Jace dropped his head into his hands. Reya sagged with exhaustion, unable to do so much as open her eyes. Instead, she breathed out a single word. "Now."

Emerson immediately bit into his wrist and placed the wound over Arie's mouth, coaxing her to swallow the life-giving blood. Tristan took Reya into the next room to replenish her, as well. Aden offered his wrist to Jace.

They continued to wait in silence, even after Emerson removed his wrist. His plea nearly broke Kate's heart. "Aurelia, come back to me. I love you, woman."

"You are my life," she responded, her voice the barest thread of sound.

The room held its breath as she lifted her lashes to gaze lovingly into her mate's eyes. After a moment they swept the room, landing first on Kate, then Jade. They were now connected, much as the shadowmen both Kate and Jade had saved.

"Thank you," she said quietly, the exhaustion plain on her face. She'd just fought a battle for her very mind, body, and soul. "Thank you all."

"How do you feel?" Reya asked as she came back into the room, her cheeks flushed with color once again. She didn't seem completely steady but managed to walk on her own.

"Tired," Arie answered. "But the pain is gone. This is incredible."

"You'll need to rest for a while. You are welcome to use our rooms."

"Your room is also ready if you felt up to being moved," Jade added.

Aurelia and Emerson exchanged a glance. "Emerson can bring me to our room. Thank you all so much. I owe you my life."

"You have incredible strength of will," Reya said. "Anyone weaker would have given over to the darkness. You remained strong for years. We did nothing compared to that."

Arie gave her a watery smile before Emerson lifted her into his arms. "I owe you a debt, regardless. Thank you," he said quietly into the room. "Aden, I know you and Arie would like to catch up. We will contact you after she's rested."

"Of course," Aden replied, kissing his sister gently on the cheek. "I'll see you soon."

Talon led them out, and Kate watched as Jade made her way over to Reya. "Could I speak with you for a moment? Privately?"

Nodding, Reya gestured for Jade to go into the adjoining room. Though curious as to what that was about, Kate knew Jade would share in time. Instead of worrying, she turned back to Hugh. "Let's get out of here for a little while, shall we?"

Hugh smiled and dipped his head in a farewell to Aden, Jace, and Tristan, who were the last to remain in the room. Clasping hands, they walked slowly down the stairs and out into the sunlight. It was a gorgeous fall day, and after what they had just gone through, Kate wanted to enjoy it.

"You're feeling all right? Healing a soul has never taken a toll before," Hugh said, obviously worried.

"It was more than healing a soul," Kate said, trying to explain what had happened. "It was like there were two souls— Arie's, and the shadowman who changed her. So, while I healed hers, we banished his together."

They'd walked into the trees surrounding the bed-and-breakfast, and Hugh paused to wrap her in his arms. Kate went willingly, knowing they both needed a moment to center themselves. His lips moved against her hair. "You are so incredible. How did I get so lucky?"

"You climbed into my trunk," she reminded him. They both laughed, and Kate pulled away to look up into his face. "So, being around all this wedding stuff, does it make you wish we had a ceremony?"

"I am already tied to you," Hugh said, "but if you wish to perform a ceremony, you know I would make that happen for you."

Turning to continue their walk through the woods, Kate thought about her answer. "Growing up, I was never the girl that dreamed about her wedding day. Boys didn't interest me."

"That's because you were waiting for your mate," Hugh said smugly.

Slapping the back of her hand lightly against his arm, Kate grinned. "You keep telling yourself that."

"Kate." Hugh said her name softly, pausing until she looked up at him. "Do you want to get married?"

"My dad would like that. Just something small?"

"With your family? And all our adopted children?"

Laughing at his term for the rescued shadowmen they'd been looking after, Kate shrugged casually. "I guess we could get married."

"You guess?"

"Tell you what," she said with a playful grin, taking a few steps away. "We'll get married...if you can catch me."

Closing her eyes, Kate pulled herself inward, willing her body to become the air itself. Once her clothes had collapsed to the ground, she re-formed until she was in the shape of a red-brown wolf. She'd been practicing this at every opportunity since her conversion. The freedom in running as an animal never got old.

Kate took off like a shot, racing away from Hugh. Paws pounded against the earth, reading messages with each step. The wind blew secrets into her ears, and her eyesight was sharp. Within moments Hugh caught her, nudging his mate's flank as they ran together through the thick woods.

Chapter 5

Valentina loved her family, but a girl needed some alone time every now and then.

After spending her whole life in the mountainous desert of their tribal land, the lush forests and green scenery of Wisconsin was a welcome change, and Valentina itched to explore.

Unfortunately, she'd somehow gotten wrapped up by some crazy female code to help with wedding plans. Wedding plans, of all things. Raven seemed to be a natural at it and clearly in her element. Even Nova and Tala seemed to be content to spend the days picking out flower arrangements and looking at tulle, but it just wasn't Valentina's cup of tea.

This morning seemed worse than the rest. She could feel the woods calling to her, begging her to explore. Valentina found the property that the Mescalero Clan stayed at absolutely beautiful, with a small lake and plenty of privacy. Talon owned quite a bit of land around the area and had already offered his extended family a place to stay anytime they wished to return.

There was a good chance Valentina would be taking him up on that offer. Not that she didn't miss her mountains, she did. They were a magical, important place for her people—but she also had the travel bug, bad.

Sneaking out early in the morning, Valentina stopped along the edge of the lake to dip her hand into its cool waters. Circles rippled out from the contact, and she watched them for a moment, feeling better now that she was out in the open, out in nature. Where she could breathe.

But it wasn't enough. Something pushed her further, inviting her into the thick trees that surrounded the property. Looking back once at the string of cabins her friends and family slept in, Valentina turned and began to walk.

As soon as she stepped into the darkened interior of the woods, a chill swept over her, and she pulled her sweatshirt tighter against her chest. Okay, she missed the heat, too. There had been frost along the ground every morning this week.

Frost.

But, if she kept up a good pace, she would remain warm. Her blood ran hotter than a normal human, anyway. Because Valentina was Gifted. Until Lani had entered their lives, Valentina and her extended family hadn't had a name for what they were. Sure, they'd all grown up with the legends of powerful, supernatural twins and medicine women who had impressive healing abilities, but who believed in that stuff?

Well, she did. Valentina had always known there was a thread of truth in the stories. She believed they all did—at least those born Gifted.

Hell, four people in her family plus four more that she considered family could shift into wolf form at will. If that didn't get a person to believe in the supernatural, Valentina didn't know what would. But then Lani came along with proof of Elementals and mates and Gifted, and suddenly, her whole life had changed.

There was so much more out there for her. It was finally time to give in to those whispers she'd ignored all those years. What was out there, she still had yet to figure out. But there was something, Valentina was sure of it.

Shivering again, Valentina stuck her hands in her pockets and continued on her trek. Her family would probably worry when they woke and discovered her gone, but she wasn't turning back now.

After a good half hour of walking and spotting deer, squirrels, and other small creatures, she heard a huff of air, way too close for comfort. This came from an animal larger than a squirrel, and much, much more dangerous than a deer.

Valentina paused, a tendril of fear snaking down her spine. Yup, it had been stupid to come out here on her own.

Staying perfectly still, she listened closely and heard the rustle of leaves just a few feet to her right. Perfectly frozen, she forced her eyes over and tried to shriek in fear, but the sound got lost as her vocal cords tensed in terror.

A huge, gray wolf stared back at her, just an arm's length away. And he looked...hungry.

"N-nice wolf," Valentina stuttered, her voice higher pitched than normal. "You don't want to eat me. I wouldn't taste very good."

Its massive head cocked to the side. Studied her. Deep gray eyes, nearly matching its fur, gazed at the terrified woman who had appeared from the mist. There was something strange about this creature. Intelligence shone from its eyes, and it had yet to attack. Energy shimmered in the air as Valentina realized, too late, why the animal seemed different.

It was no animal. The wolf disappeared as a human form glimmered into existence. Those same piercing gray eyes glittered down at her, dark hair falling in easy waves against a pair of broad shoulders.

I beg to differ, came the words inside her head. *I think you would taste very good.*

With another gasp, she stumbled back, shock from the voice sending her gaze to drift away from those eyes...and trail down a very nude body.

"Oh, jeez," she cried out, spinning away and covering her eyes. "You're naked."

"Does my bare skin bother you?" he asked aloud, his voice full of amusement.

"Yes!" she practically screamed. It was a lie, of course. It was taking all her control not to turn back and drink him in, in all his glory. Shrugging out of her sweatshirt, Valentina held it out in offering. "Here, take this and cover up."

"It's all right; I'm covered."

Not fully trusting that statement, she peeked out of one eye before turning fully around. Somehow, he had pulled on a pair of cotton pants—though that still left his top bare, and she couldn't help but salivate as her eyes traced each delicious muscle. Dragging her gaze back to his face, Valentina offered a stiff nod. "That's...better."

"My name is Embry Jain," he announced, bowing at the waist. His strange manners had her mouth hanging open. When she remained silent, he prompted, "And you are?"

"Valentina," she answered him after another moment. "Valentina Stone."

Embry scooped her free hand into a kiss. His hot touch sent electrical currents along her skin. He practically purred her name. "Valentina. A pleasure."

Pulling her hand away with a snap, Valentina began to back away again. Sure, this guy was dead sexy and charming to boot, but who the hell was he? An Elemental, obviously, but it was like he was taking over her every sense. She needed to breathe, to think. Neither of those could happen with him around.

He watched her with confusion as she slowly backed away. Those intense eyes tracked her every movement. "Where are you going?"

"Home. I mean, where I'm staying. Back to my family." Away from you, she added to herself.

"But I've only just found you."

"Yeah, well, I wasn't trying to be found."

"I don't understand. I can feel our connection. Do you not feel it as well?" This terrifying, strange pull that felt like she was being sucked under the strong current of a river? Oh yeah, she felt it. "You're frightened. I apologize, I did not mean to startle you. Your presence startled me."

"My presence?"

"Yes, Valentina. You are my mate. I never thought I would find you."

"Ha!" She let out a loud guffaw, her nerves shot. His *mate*? "I don't think so."

"You weren't surprised by my ability to shift from wolf to man. You know of Elemental existence. You yourself are Gifted, are you not?"

Still backing away, Valentina held out a palm to halt him. "Look, this is all new to me. Mates and Elementals and Gifted. Can we just back up a little?"

"All right," he said, remaining perfectly still. "What can I do to help you?"

Pausing in her retreat, leaving several feet between them, Valentina took a breath. "Let's start at the beginning. Where did you come from?"

"Just now, or since the beginning of my existence?"

Oh, man. His existence? That didn't bode well. "Let's start with just now and work our way back."

"As you wish," he said, inclining his head. She struggled not to roll her eyes. "I am with a group of Elementals who have arrived to celebrate the union of Talon Wolfchild and Jade Callaghan. Talon offered us a place to stay along Black Bear Lake."

Valentina knew where that was—it was the property lining Talon and Jade's. That cleared up some things. "Okay, good. Talon is my...extended family."

"You are from the Mescalero Tribe?" he asked, obviously well-informed.

"That's right. How do you know Talon and Jade?"

"Jade...saved me," he replied, seeming hesitant to reveal this piece of information.

"Saved you?" Valentina's eyebrows knit together as she worked through this. The light dawned almost instantly. "You're one of the former shadowmen."

"That's correct," he answered, his eyes suddenly pained. "And because of that, I know I will never truly deserve you. You are pure goodness, pure light. I can see it plainly, burning brightly through your eyes. If you decide you do not want me, I will understand and leave you."

Her heart jumped at his words, then dropped as his last statement hit harder than expected. She'd known him all of five minutes; why did the thought of him leaving give her palpitations? "Okay, we don't need to go to any extremes yet. Why don't we get to know each other first?"

His lips spread into a full smile, easily rivaling the sun. The beauty of it took her breath away. He held out his hand, palm up, for her to take. "Walk with me?"

"All right," she answered, reaching out to accept the offer. "But first, we're finding you some clothes."

Chapter 6

As they left Arie's room, Reese hugged her arms against her stomach and smiled at Dominic. "I'm so glad Arie is all right. Thank goodness that she agreed to come here."

"I'm happy also, but you have been too stressed out. That can't be good for the babies. Do you need anything?"

"I *am* hungry." Dominic had been overprotective before they found out that they were expecting—now, he was almost insufferable.

Almost. It was a good thing Reese loved him more than life itself.

"What would you like?"

"Pizza." As if he even had to ask. It was all she'd been craving. Reese blamed it on the fact that they'd eaten pizza the night they'd first...created life.

"Of course," he said with a grin. "I hope the restaurant in town serves it."

"Let's walk down there and find out. This is just the cutest little town."

They strolled out of the bed-and-breakfast, having handed the twins back to their parents and checked briefly on Arie. She needed time to rest. Even Emerson needed to recover. He had shared his strength with his mate to fight off the shadow of Maurice, and it had taken a toll on them both.

Reese and Dominic made their way to Main Street, where the only sit-down restaurant in town resided. Simply called the Log Cabin, it had been decorated with that in mind.

"Have you thought any more about where you would like to raise the children?" Dominic asked. It was a point of dissension between them—Reese loved traveling and thought they could continue to do so when the babies were born. Dominic thought children needed a place to call home. It was a nice idea, so she'd been attempting to compromise.

"Now that Arie's found her brother, do you think she'll want to go to New Zealand with him?"

"I'm not sure, why?"

"Well, I know you'll want to stay close to your brother. Maybe we should discuss this as a group."

"Reese." Dominic said her name with a wealth of love. "We will make our home where we want. I would prefer to have my brother near, but that will ultimately be his decision."

Thinking about that, Reese finally said, "I really like it around here. Or Duluth, I wouldn't mind going back."

It was where they had met, after all. And she'd made some good friends there. They would have gone there before the wedding, but Arie and Emerson's grave injuries had put them out of commission for longer than expected.

"If that is what you want, that is what we will do," Dominic replied, bringing their joined hands to his mouth to nibble along her knuckles.

"Can we call it a home base, instead? I really would still like to travel, but I like the idea of having somewhere to go back to."

"Of course; I still have my property there. We can expand our home to include a nursery. There's enough land to build guest homes, if Emerson and Arie would like to stay, along with Edith and Anya. Or more, if her brother wants to be near."

Excitement jumbled in Reese's stomach. Having made the decision, she suddenly felt lighter. "That sounds perfect! Oh, man, Jordan and Gabi will be so excited."

The two friends she'd made working at a retail store stayed in constant contact. They both now knew the truth about her—not the Elemental part, but that Reese was actually a writer and had been working overnight retail shifts for a story.

Neither of them begrudged her the lie, and they'd grown close even over long-distance. "Speaking of, isn't Gabi—"

"Reese!" A voice shrieked from across the street, cutting Dominic off from his question.

Reese turned with a wide grin, spotting Gabi as she made a mad dash across the road. Her heart leaped in her throat as a car slammed on its brakes at the last minute. *You would have saved her, right?*

Yes, Dominic answered, though she could hear the sigh in his words.

Gabi attacked her with a hug, then instantly stepped back and placed a hand against Reese's stomach. "Oh no, are they okay?"

"Yes," Reese said with a laugh. "I'm not that fragile."

She launched herself at Dominic next, forcing him into a hug. He took it manfully, though he sent Reese a grimace behind her back. "It's so good to see you! Where are you headed?"

"Grabbing some lunch. Want to join?"

"Sure! I just got to town, and I'll be finding Pearl later." The friends linked arms, and Reese made sure to grab Dominic's hand before they left him behind.

"Have you seen your family yet?" Gabi had grown up here, escaping to the bigger city for college.

"I'm staying with my parents. I dropped my bags off and said hi. Dom, where's your brother? I wanted to meet him."

"His girlfriend isn't feeling well," Dominic said in a smooth stretch of truth, "so he'll be around once she's feeling better."

"That's too bad! I hope she's all right."

"She will be," he replied with assurance.

"I want to hear all about your Europe trip. How exciting!"

Dominic and Reese shared a grin as they reached the restaurant. He opened the door for the ladies, and Reese took the opportunity to kiss his cheek as they stepped into the main room. *You owe me for this.*

Reese sent him a wink filled with dark promises. *You know I always pay up.*

They grabbed a table and placed their order as Gabi filled Reese in on gossip from the store and asked nonstop questions about their trip. Pushing back from the table, Reese gazed at the two pizzas they'd devoured between the three of them. The babies were happy, settled for the moment, and she felt stuffed.

Reese had told Gabi what she could—the beauty of the countryside in Romania, the stunning old cities in Russia. What she left out included the battles with shadowmen and the near-death experiences they'd all had.

"So, we have some news," Reese began at a break in Gabi's rambling. Clasping her hand over Dominic's, she grinned widely. "We're moving back to Duluth."

"What?" Her squeal had several tables full of people turning their heads. "No way, that's amazing!" Gabi jumped up to wrap Reese in another hug, then as an afterthought, she slung one arm around Dominic, too. Reese found she'd missed Gabi's exuberance while they'd been away. "Oh, man, I'm so excited! I can't wait to spoil your babies rotten. I'm going to be the best aunt ever."

Laughing, Reese squeezed her back. "They'll need that, with as overprotective as Dominic will be."

"Do you know what you're having yet?" Gabi asked, pulling away just enough to make eye contact.

In fact, Reese had known for quite some time but had wanted to wait to tell her in person. "Both girls."

Gabi squealed again, gripping Reese's hands and jumping up and down. "Oh, Dom, get ready for lots of pink and lace and rainbows!"

"My daughters will be strong and fierce and will have no time for such trappings."

Gabi and Reese both giggled, and Reese stage-whispered to her with a wink. "He's going to be such a pushover."

"I can hear you," Dominic replied drily.

"Oh, I know," Reese said, reaching over to give him a wet kiss on the cheek. "And you know I speak the truth."

They left the restaurant since Gabi had promised to meet up with Pearl, and Dominic and Reese wanted to check in again with Arie. After that, Reese wanted to visit with Edith and Anya. Now that Arie had successfully rid herself of Maurice's influence, Reese wondered if the other two women would be willing to try.

Their group had kept Edith and Anya a secret for the time being. Reese hadn't even told Reya or Jade about them since they were still reeling from everything they'd been through in their lives. Anya had yet to open up about what had happened to her before being kidnapped by Maurice, and their group respected her right to keep it to herself.

Reese hoped, one day, that she would feel comfortable enough with someone to talk about it. She couldn't even imagine the demons Anya must battle on a daily basis.

Still, it didn't diminish her joy of life. There were times Anya had such a sweet innocence in her face as she practically devoured new knowledge and experiences. There seemed to be no fear in that girl. Then, she would say something so wise and beyond her years, and her eyes would take on an ageless look that was all too reticent of the terrors of her past.

Reese got on well with Anya since Reese's thirst for knowledge rivaled hers. Edith tended to be a little more reserved, and for good reason. She'd had very little outside contact in her time as Maurice's prisoner. She'd barely known another life existed before she had been ripped away from her home and family.

Yet, she was the reason Arie'd been able to hold on in those dark times. She'd reminded Arie of what life could be. And now, there was every possibility all three of them could live it, without pain.

What are you thinking about? Dominic asked privately.

They were walking back toward the bed-and-breakfast, hand in hand. Looking up at his beloved face, Reese answered. *Arie, Edith, and Anya. I'm hoping Edith and Anya allow Reya, Jade, and Kate to help them.*

Those three are stronger than any of us. It will not be an easy thing, but I believe they will.

When they reached the inn, Reese and Dominic went straight to Emerson and Arie's room. Dominic had already spoken to Emerson using their telepathic link, making sure they were ready for visitors. Dominic knocked; the door opened quickly to reveal Emerson. The heaviness under Emerson's eyes was already gone, though he still needed more rest. The brothers clasped arms, sharing a moment of pure joy now that the truth had managed to sink in a bit.

Stepping fully into the room, Reese spotted Arie on the bed, her brother at her side. She felt so incredibly happy for them both. Reese couldn't imagine the pain they must have felt at thinking they'd been lost to the other all these years.

"Hi, Arie. How are you feeling?"

She cracked a smile. "Better. I'd forgotten what it's like to live without pain. I feel light, happy. It's amazing."

Aden smiled at Reese, then held out a hand. "We weren't properly introduced earlier. I'm Aden."

"Reese. And Dominic, Emerson's brother and my mate."

The men clasped hands as the brothers joined them around the bed. Arie pinched the comforter between two fingers as she looked back at Reese.

"I've spoken with Edith and Anya," she said. Stealing a glance at her brother, she added, "I've told Aden about them. I'm hoping they'll both decide to meet with the healers. I want this for them."

"We were planning on visiting them next," Reese said. "I'll see how they're feeling about it."

"Thank you."

"There's something else we wanted to discuss," Reese said, including Aden and Emerson. "Dominic and I have decided to settle in Duluth, and we'd like you all to stay with us."

Something passed between Emerson and Arie, while Reese noticed Aden's eyes drifting somewhere outside this room. She didn't know anything about the man and wasn't sure if this was something he would want.

"Emerson and I would love to stay," Arie said. "And I'm sure Edith and Anya will, as well. They've no desire to return to Europe."

Aden looked down at his sister, studying her for a long time. So many emotions passed over his features, it was difficult to name them. "I'd like to stay with you. I've only just found you; I won't let you go so easily."

Her lips spread into a wide grin as she clasped her brother's hand to her chest. "I'd love that. Are you certain, though? I know you've made a home in New Zealand."

"It will still be there for me. I can go visit, and they all can come here."

Reese felt like she was missing an important detail in this conversation but decided not to press it for now. Moving in to hug Arie, she couldn't help the sting of tears hovering against her lids. "Sorry. Baby hormones. We're going to see Edith and Anya now."

"Talk to them," Arie said.

Reese understood the deeper meaning behind her words. "I'll do my best."

Chapter 7

Standing on the small porch, Edith took a deep breath just because she could. Simply breathing in the fresh air had done wonders for her health and her psyche. She hoped, one day, she'd be able to stand in the sun without burning.

Anya dug in the earth under the shade of an oak tree, planting bulbs that would bloom brilliantly in the springtime. Even though they'd only rented this place for the week, she felt the need to beautify it somehow. To leave her mark.

She had been such a bright, sunny spot in Edith's life. Hers and Arie's, not to mention Reese and the Drake brothers. Anya had been through so much as just a child that it broke Edith's heart. Edith knew more than Anya had been willing to speak about—sometimes her special gift could be so intrusive—but Edith kept it to herself until Anya felt ready to open up.

They'd just heard from Arie, and Edith couldn't even describe how full her heart felt that she had been healed. It gave her hope—it gave them all hope. And though she still felt anxious around others, Edith knew she would allow these miracle women to attempt a healing.

Not just the women. Jace, too. Oh, she would have to face that music sooner rather than later.

Edith had spent so much time reassuring Arie that life was worth living, that one day she would escape the evil clutches of Maurice, but Edith never truly considered that future for herself. She'd always believed she would die making sure Arie felt freedom once again.

Edith didn't want to be afraid of it now, but she had many years of repression to work through. One baby step at a time. Jace had been nothing but kind and patient with her, even as Edith knew his baser instincts encouraged him to claim his mate. Her.

Settling into the comfortable porch swing, Edith picked up a history book she'd been muddling through while Anya worked in the yard. Edith had learned some reading before she'd been captured, but that was many moons ago. In all the years of being a prisoner, she'd yearned for knowledge, for learning. Arie and Reese—and even Dominic and Emerson—had been so patient with her and with Anya. Reese especially sat with them both for hours on end, teaching them to read and write as if they were children. She never made either of them feel inadequate or laughed at their endless questions. If she hadn't already found her calling as an author, she would have made an amazing teacher.

She would definitely make a wonderful mother. Edith couldn't wait for her babies to be born; she couldn't remember a time in her life that she'd held a baby or played with a child. It would be a new experience, for certain. Not just for Edith. For Arie and Anya as well.

Edith heard a car approaching long before it arrived. It was easy to distinguish the tread of the tire against the gravel drive, and she stood to greet Reese and Dominic as they came into view. Cars, fast trains, planes—they'd terrified Edith at first. Still did, if she could be honest with herself. So much had changed from her girlhood to the present. So much technology, knowledge, available at her fingertips. Between catching up on her education and the daily Elemental practice, Edith hardly had any downtime.

That suited her fine, most days. Too many years had been spent alone.

Anya danced across the lawn to hug Reese. She talked animatedly about her garden work as they all came up to the house. Anya's large, floppy hat covered her between the shady patch of trees until she joined Edith on the covered porch.

Edith accepted Reese's hug and clasped Dominic's arms in greeting. He didn't frighten her anymore. Emerson and Dominic both had been open and honest, willing to not only allow her to read them but also to do anything in their power to protect her and Anya. They saw the two women like the sisters they'd never had. Edith saw them as her kin.

"How is Arie?"

Though Edith had spoken to Arie on the cellphone—a contraption Anya felt much more at ease with than Edith did—she knew Arie would put on a brave front no matter what had happened. She wanted to hear it from Reese. "She's resting, but she looks so good. The three women went to battle for her. Jace, too."

On hearing his name, Edith's pulse sped. Reese flicked her a look but didn't comment any further. Edith knew Jace had been there to help. She'd felt it. Much like when he'd examined Arie on his own back in Russia and he'd been snared by Maurice's evil stench. She'd felt it then, too. Felt compelled to find him, connect with him and lead him out of the trap Maurice had left. Had done the same this day.

Just because she didn't feel ready for a mate relationship didn't mean she would allow Jace to suffer.

Anya's bright smile helped to settle her nerves. "This is wonderful news! Can we see her? Can these women help us?"

"I believe the answer to both of those is yes," Reese said. "But it's up to the two of you. I know you're not feeling comfortable enough to join the festivities, but would you be willing to have Reya, Jade, and Kate come here?"

Anya looked at Edith, her heart in her eyes. Edith knew Anya had held back from meeting the others because of her. And she would continue to do so unless Edith stepped up. The thought of being in a crowd like that rendered her catatonic, but having the three women come to them? To that, she could agree.

"Ask them to come here," Edith said. "We would very much appreciate that."

Anya couldn't contain her excitement. She wrapped her arms around Edith's neck. "Spasibo, Edith!"

When Anya released her, Edith took her hands. "You should go back with them. I know you want to meet everyone."

"I won't leave you here alone."

"I am safe, and I have plenty to keep me occupied. If something happens, I can reach out with that," Edith said, gesturing toward the mobile device. "This is important to you. I do not want you to hold back on my account."

"Show me you know how to make a call, and I go."

Not one to back down from a challenge, Edith picked up the smooth screen and pressed the button to make it light up. Touching the green button that had a picture of a phone, Edith found Reese's name, watched as the word *calling* floated across the screen.

Music went off in Reese's bag, and she nodded approvingly. "I think you're good."

Anya crossed her arms and frowned. "We will put up a barrier."

"Feel free. I have nowhere to go."

It seemed like Anya ran out of arguments. She flashed a smile at Reese and Dominic before bounding into the house. "I will change, and then we go."

Reese sank into the swing and patted the seat beside her. Edith joined her, picking up the thick book she'd been reading and placing it on her lap. "There's something else we wanted to talk to you about. Dominic and I have decided to stay in Duluth. We spoke to Emerson and Arie, along with her brother. They'd like to join us."

"Then we will, also."

"I don't want you to feel like you have to," Reese began, but Edith waved off her concern.

"You are our family now, as I am certain Anya will agree." From inside the house, they all heard an affirmative. "We go where you go. I have never seen this part of the world. It is beautiful and feels safe. One day we may leave, go somewhere else. For now, I am happy here."

"Me too," Anya agreed, stepping out in a pair of jeans rolled to the ankle with a pale-yellow floral top that Reese had called a gypsy blouse. The sleeves puffed out on top but met just above her wrist with a cinch that created fun ruffles. The buttons down the front were shaped like flowers, the fabric broken up by a strip of wide lace across her belly button before the bottom hem flared out.

Anya had a sense of style Edith feared she would never catch up with. She'd grown up wearing corsets and uncomfortably large skirts. Even now, she tended to wear long skirts—Reese called them maxis—and tops that covered most of her skin. Unless they were practicing, then Edith opted for cotton pants.

"Enjoy yourself, and don't worry about me."

Anya blew Edith a kiss and danced to the car. Reese moved slower, and Edith worried something might be wrong with the babies. When she said as much, Reese waved her off. "More like pizza babies. I ate too much at lunch."

"If you are certain." After a pause, Edith added, "Watch over Anya. I fear she does not take enough precautions."

"Will do." Reese winked, then leaned over to kiss her on the cheek. "Enjoy some peace and quiet."

Edith watched as they piled into the car and kicked up bits of gravel while Dominic steered it expertly down the drive. Though she put on a brave face, Edith preferred walking or horseback to those metal contraptions. Perhaps there would be enough land for a horse or two in Duluth. Joy rose at the prospect.

Opening the book in her lap, Edith lost herself in the battle of Gettysburg and reread Lincoln's speech on freedom. What a precious thing that seemed to be taken for granted by those that had it. She vowed to remember this gift every single day.

The sun reached its apex as Edith continued to sit and study. Though she remained protected on the porch, its proximity had her moving inside to wait out the hottest part of the day. She tidied the already immaculate space before fixing herself some tea and curling up in one of the comfortable, overstuffed chairs. She had never felt such luxury in her life.

Deciding she had studied enough for the day, Edith took a small book from its hiding spot and found the worn bookmark to indicate where she'd left off. The cover depicted a shirtless man on a windswept beach, holding onto his beloved, who wore nothing more than a chemise. Looking at the artwork too long made Edith blush, but she'd found she highly enjoyed the steamy romance.

She just didn't tell anyone else about them. It felt too personal. Too embarrassing.

The day, the heat must have gotten to her, for Edith's eyes slipped closed, and she found herself standing on a beach in a scandalously revealing white dress. She glanced behind her and found Jace taking long strides to her side, the muscles of his chest gleaming through the opening of his white shirt, unbuttoned nearly to his navel. The simple brown pants he wore had been tucked into tall, black leather boots. He looked like a swashbuckling pirate, only missing his parrot and sword.

Edith went willingly into his arms, and he kissed her with a vigor that seemed purely fictional. When she finally came up for breath, his lips trailed down her neck and set her blood alight with what could only be lust.

Closing her eyes to enjoy the new and terrifying sensation, Edith felt his mouth move up her throat and to her ear. His whispered words sent chills down her spine.

"Hello, pet."

Edith pulled away, but Maurice was too strong. His shock-blue eyes laughed down at her. His mouth split into an evil grin, his fangs dripping with the bright red blood of his most recent kill.

Edith felt trapped. Helpless. He sank his teeth into her neck, and she let loose with a shrill scream that echoed to the heavens and back.

Sitting up with a start, Edith pressed a palm to her pounding heart and willed her breath back to normal. Tears streamed down her cheeks as she struggled to differentiate between the here and now and the horrible nightmare.

Without thinking, she reached out to Jace. His presence instantly soothed her frayed nerves.

Edith? What's happened?

Nothing. It was nothing.

I feel your fear, your anxiety. Are you in danger? I will come to you.

No. For a moment, she closed her eyes and enjoyed the comfort of his voice. It was only a bad dream.

I ran into Anya with Reese and Dominic. I introduced her to my friends that I grew up with. Would you like company? He paused, then added, *It doesn't have to be me.*

Thank you for your concern, but I assure you I am fine. Dominic and Reese set a protection barrier before they left, and I am not without defenses.

I know that, but I can do none other than worry. That is my cross to bear, not yours. He paused again, hoping she would bring up the healing session she'd agreed to try. When she didn't, he ventured, *Anya said you were both to meet with Reya, Jade, and Kate.*

Guilt swept through Edith, though she didn't fully understand why. *I was going to tell you.*

You owe me nothing.

That's not true. This time she paused, forcing herself to say the next words. *I would like you to be there.*

Are you certain?

I would not ask were there any doubt in my mind.

Then I will be there. I will do anything in my power to eradicate Maurice from your life...I only wish I could have done something sooner.

Only then did Edith realize that Jace blamed himself for her capture. What a ridiculous notion, yet it warmed her in ways she'd never felt before. *We were a world apart. You have not let me down, Jace. I do not know that you ever could.*

He didn't answer for a while. Edith opened her mind to him and was hit with overwhelming emotions, a conglomeration which she couldn't begin to decipher. *Thank you for speaking with me. All vestiges of the dream have dissipated.*

You are too kind, taku tama muna.

His beloved. She didn't deserve the name.

Chapter 8

Early this morning, Lenna had watched Valentina sneak away from the house she stayed in with her brother and Raven. She looked on edge, like a caged tiger. Lenna understood perfectly.

The truth was, Lenna had been feeling that way since Wynne had walked into her life. Elementals, daemons, mates—it could all be a bit overwhelming sometimes.

Thankfully, Wynne understood her need to take things slow. Lenna imagined time moved differently for someone who had been on this earth, or any world, as long as he had. That freaked her out. A lot of it freaked her out.

Yet, whenever Lenna looked at him, her pulse began to race. Whenever she felt anxious, she'd reach out on their mental path, and he'd be there to soothe her frayed nerves. Lenna couldn't imagine her life now without him in it. So, what was her problem?

I'm going for a run. Want to join?

Her brother always had perfect timing. Elan could sense her edginess, too. He blamed it on Wynne, but his reasoning differed from Lenna's. *Meet you at the tree line.*

Not bothering with the door, Lenna lifted the window of her main floor room and straddled the sill. Elan came around the corner, already in wolf form, and turned his massive head with his tongue lolling out in a wolfy smirk. Taking that as a challenge, Lenna shimmied out of her pajamas and left them in a heap on the ground.

They'd been running together as wolves since she could remember. Shifting between forms had been second nature, though they'd hidden the talent from others, including their own family. The only ones who had known had been their mom and uncle since they possessed the same ability. They'd kept a close eye on their children for the signs. Just after Lenna and Elan had turned five, they'd been climbing trees in the hills surrounding the reservation. Lenna slipped and fell, landing on all fours. Elan had gone after her, and the shock of the fall had him turning as well.

They'd been speaking telepathically as long as they could remember. Even before they could form actual words, they had a twin connection that was unbreakable. They kept to themselves. Kept each other's secrets.

After Lani's recent visit and the subsequent daemon attack, the wolf was now out of the bag.

In less than a second, Lenna had given herself over to her inner animal. The transformation felt at once as if she were falling from a cliff and wearing a jetpack under the water. Her body contorted until she could feel the soft ground beneath her paws. Lenna didn't wait; launching off her powerful back legs, she shot toward the trees like a bullet.

Elan, while larger and more powerful, also tended to be slower. Lenna managed to catch him just as he reached the thickest part of the wood. Together they bounded over broken tree limbs, splashed through freezing streams, and kicked up enough fall leaves for a photo shoot. It felt good to let themselves go. She'd needed that release.

Ready to head back? Elan asked. Lenna had a feeling he wanted breakfast; her own stomach rumbled.

Care to wager?

Last one there makes pancakes.

You're on, Lenna said as she sprang forward. This time, while she went over and around obstacles, Elan tore his way straight through, thinking that would give him the advantage. He was wrong. She saved her last burst of speed for when they emerged from the woods, skidding to a stop just past the door.

Cheater.

How?

I don't know, but I swear it.

"Well done," came a voice from the porch. Lenna nearly transformed back into her human form in surprise. *It's all right if you want to shift. I will make sure you're covered.*

Taking Wynne up on his offer, Lenna released her wolf and pulled herself back to two legs. Wynne asked the earth to provide his mate with cotton pants and shirt, similar to her pajamas. She loved that trick. "Thank you. What are you doing here?"

Before he could answer, Elan shifted. Wynne must have fashioned pants for him, as well. Lenna appreciated it, even if Elan didn't care. "Yeah. What are you doing here?"

"I wished to speak with Lenna."

Lenna looked over at her brother, who stood just feet from Wynne with his arms crossed. Though Elan towered over her, he didn't come close to Wynne's height. "It's all right. You can get those pancakes started."

After another few seconds of glaring, Elan sauntered into the house. Wynne and Lenna stood awkwardly on the porch. She wanted to meet his gaze, but doing so always made her a little bit dizzy. She preferred to have all her faculties when they talked.

"We have not spoken since arriving. How do you like the area?"

"I like it. Not to stay in forever, but the woods are a nice change. My wolf enjoys running through them."

"Perhaps we could go running together."

Finally, she met his gaze. Lenna could feel his eyes on her, studying her every expression. The truth was, she loved looking at Wynne. It just made it difficult to think. Or breathe. "I'd like that."

"Tonight? Eight o'clock?"

"We could eat something, too," Lenna said, offering a small olive branch. It was the most forward she'd been in the relationship thus far. "I could cook."

"I would like that very much," he said, scooping up her hand to place his lips against her knuckles. "Until then."

Her heart thumped hard in her chest. This daemon was potent.

As Wynne walked down the porch and into the thick trees, Lenna stood and watched him go. Unfortunately, she didn't have as much privacy as she'd thought. *If you're done making googly eyes, I could use some help in here.*

Lenna turned to look through the window with a glare, her brother leaning back from the kitchen to peer out the front. He grinned, unrepentant, before moving back to his task. With a little sigh, she joined him inside.

"It's about time," Elan groused. "What did that guy want, anyway?"

"Me," Lenna mumbled, just quiet enough to evade his sharp ears. When he opened his mouth to ask her to repeat, she spoke louder. "He asked me to go running tonight."

"Running, at night? With a daemon?"

"With my mate."

Elan turned, spatula in hand, to look at her fully. His thick eyebrows rose in surprise. "That's the first time you've called him that."

"Doesn't make it any less true, does it?"

"What's gotten into you? Did that daemon say something to you?"

Rolling her eyes, Lenna banged a palm against the counter. "His name is Wynne. Not that guy, or that daemon. Wynne."

"You're acting weird."

"Of course I am! Four months ago, I was living a completely normal life, and now I'm mated to a daemon and my brother is being a giant jerk! How do you expect me to act?"

"Lenna, chill," Elan began, but she'd had enough.

"No, you need to chill. I'm not hungry."

Turning, she stormed off to her room and slammed the door shut. Stupid, annoying brothers. Sinking onto the edge of the bed, Lenna dropped her head and took deep breaths. If she could be honest with herself for a moment, she'd know Elan had nothing to do with it. This was all on her.

Her first date with Wynne had gone so well. He'd shown up with flowers at her work and invited her to lunch. After their first awkward small talk, they'd both managed to loosen up and discovered they had more in common than Lenna ever could have imagined. He'd brought her back to work, kissed her hand just like he'd done on the porch, and went on his way.

She'd gone back to work floating on a cloud. Then reality sank in.

A hesitant knock on the door interrupted her thoughts. Before she could accept or deny the intrusion, Elan pushed open the door and sat beside her. "I'm sorry, Lenna."

"For which part?"

"All of it. I haven't been very supportive. I only acted that way because it seemed like you weren't interested in him."

"Well, I am."

Elan sighed. "I know. And that wasn't the only reason—I was also a little jealous. We've done everything together since we were born. I didn't want to lose you."

Lenna looked up at her brother. That was the most vulnerable she'd ever heard him be. "Elan, I'd never let anyone come between us. Even a mate."

"Things will be different, though."

"Of course they will. Things are bound to be different. We're adults now. Your mate will be out there somewhere, too. What do you think will happen then?"

He scrunched up his face. "I can wait for that. Seriously, though, what's wrong? Why are you pushing Wynne away if you're actually interested?"

It was the first time Elan had used his name directly. Points for her brother. "I'm only twenty-three. I feel like I've barely lived. You and I had so many plans. To travel, to protect wild wolves, to have salacious love affairs with European men."

"I think that last part was just you."

"But you get my point. We haven't done any of it. I haven't. I guess I'm afraid, too. I'm afraid of disappearing into Wynne before I even have a chance to by myself."

"That won't happen."

"How do you know?"

"Because that guy is head over heels for you. Any moron can see that," he said, gesturing to himself. "He wants you to be you, and I'd bet if you wanted to travel the world, he'd take you on his private jet. The salacious love affairs might be out, though."

Allowing a small smile to show, Lenna nodded. "I don't think I'd be very good at having multiple lovers, anyway."

"Stop there, because I don't need nightmares." Elan wrapped his arm around her back and squeezed. "If Wynne is who you want to be with, I support you all the way."

It felt as if a weight had lifted. "Thanks, bro. Could you support me by letting me have the house to myself tonight?"

"Ugh, fine. I just don't want details."

"Deal. Let's go finish breakfast—I'm starved."

Chapter 9

As Dominic pulled away from the house, Anya watched Edith sitting serenely on the porch with her book on her lap and worried. Not so much about her physically. Anya knew Edith could handle herself. Dominic and Emerson and Arie all taught them well when it came to defending themselves. But for her mental and emotional well-being?

One battered and bruised soul could recognize another. Her whole life, Anya had had nothing. She didn't remember her parents. The bad men took her and raised her. Not as one would raise a cherished daughter. As one would treat a piece of property. An investment, they liked to call her and the others. They put food in their bellies and gave them a dirty mattress to sleep on at night, in a room filled with other orphans who had nowhere to go. Who had no hope. No joy.

At first in that awful place, Anya sought out comfort with the older girls, but none was to be found. For a while, she tried to give it but quickly learned that such actions angered the bad men. Instead, she created a private place they could never reach. A secret space in her mind reserved for happy, sunny thoughts. For love, for joy. She put every scrap of it that existed inside her and locked it inside that piece of her mind for safekeeping. Swore that one day she would escape and be able to unlock it again.

The bad men used her body and shattered her spirit, but they never reached that part of Anya's mind.

"She'll be all right," Reese said from the front seat. She had turned to face Anya and saw the crease between her brows. "She just needs more time."

"We have time, but I don't want her to miss out on living while we wait."

With a nod of understanding, Reese turned back to the road. Dominic captured her hand, and Anya could sense them speaking telepathically. She wondered what that kind of connection would be like if she ever found her mate. Would she feel restricted? Exposed? Would that be a good thing or a terrible one?

Deciding she didn't want to find out anytime soon, Anya turned her attention to the sights of the small town they drove through. Sun Valley. A strange name for the overcast, flat land. The sun had been out that morning, but she'd learned that the clouds always found their way across the sky at some point during the day.

Their first stop was at the bed-and-breakfast, where many of the mated pairs were staying. Anya's face brightened on seeing all the flowers in a riot of fall colors scattered along the ground. She pushed open the door before Dominic had even parked, careful to adjust her hat before stepping into the sunlight.

The whir of activity had Anya turning in a slow circle in order to soak it all in. She didn't feel afraid here. She knew if a bad man showed up that she would have many defenders. Not to mention that she could defend herself now. She was no longer a scared child.

"This is wonderful," she said to Reese when the other woman stepped out of the car. "These are all Elementals, yes?"

"Mostly. We still try to keep a low profile, though, since the owners of the bed-and-breakfast are human. As is anyone else living in town."

"Look, babies!" Anya said with a delighted clap. Before Reese could stop her, she dashed off to the field of what had once only been grass and now teemed with wildflowers. Two children sat in the center of the field, playing in the earth. Anya crouched down to join them. "Privet, malyshkas. Oh, I just want to nibble your little fingers off."

"We'd rather they keep their fingers," said a woman with more than a hint of amusement. "Hi, I'm Reya. I don't believe we've met."

"Reya!" With her characteristic enthusiasm, Anya jumped up and wrapped her arms around the other woman. "You are miracle woman. I'm so happy to meet you."

Reese hurried to smooth introductions over. "Reya, this is Anya. Sorry, I should have warned you we were coming."

"Not at all, but I'm sensing a story here."

"There is that. Anya, along with another woman, were both held by the same shadowman as Arie."

Reya gasped, concern instantly lighting her eyes. She looked at Anya, who had already crouched again to pinch Leia's cheeks and make her giggle. "You made these grow, didn't you tavitochik? Such a talented malyshka."

Tristan joined his mate's side. "What can we do to help?"

"Edith and Anya have both agreed to be examined if you're willing."

"Of course," Reya said instantly. "I'm sure Jade and Kate will feel the same."

Anya stood again, beaming at the healer. "Thank you. I have not lived with it so long, but Edith has. Please help her first."

"We will do what we can," Reya said, clasping Anya's hands. "Let me call Jade and Kate. We might all need some time to recoup from this morning."

"Yes. That will be good. Spasibo."

Reese looked at Tristan and Reya both. "Edith isn't comfortable around others yet, so if we could keep her existence lowkey until she decides to meet anyone, that would be great."

"She is under our protection as well," Tristan said. "May I ask, how long was she held?"

The pained expression crossing Reese's face said plenty. Dominic stepped in to answer. "More than a century."

Reya let out a sound of heartache, clasping her hand over her mouth. Tristan wrapped an arm around her waist, his face warping in sympathetic pain. "We will do everything we can for her. For you both."

With her bright smile, Anya nodded and looked to her left. "Jace!"

"Hello," Jace said as he approached. "Are you all right out here, Anya?"

"Oh, yes. My hat is working well. I came to meet everyone; can you introduce me to your friends?"

"Sure," Jace said, extending his arm. He nodded to Dominic, letting him know Anya would be taken care of. "You've already met Tristan—let's see if we can find the others I grew up with."

"Jared and Hugh, yes?"

"That's right. Lani, too. Tristan's sister."

"This is wonderful. So many happy people."

"Is Edith all right?"

"Yes, of course." Anya paused, gripping Jace's bicep until he looked at her. "She has agreed to meet with the miracle women. And before I come here with Reese, I made sure she know how to use the phone. I would not leave her unprotected."

"I would never think that," Jace assured her. "I only hoped she would feel comfortable enough to come into town, that's all."

Anya relaxed, then pointed at two dark-haired men she recognized from Jace's description. "Is that Hugh and Jared?"

"It is. Come on, let's go say hi."

Anya skipped over to the group with her bright smile instantly charming both men and Kate, who stood discussing their plans for the evening. Kate extended her hand first, but Anya bypassed that and went in for a hug. "You are a miracle. Thank you for healing Arie."

"It was my pleasure. What's your name?"

"Anya. I come from Russia, where the bad man found me. You will help me, yes?"

"Of course. I'm so happy to meet you, though I wish it were in better circumstances. You've already spoken to Reya?" Kate asked, looking at Jace.

"We've just come from there." His eyes flicked to Anya and back again. "There's another woman who requires your assistance. She does not wish to be part of the group festivities just yet."

Hugh and Jared both cocked their heads at the tone of Jace's voice. A silent, mutual understanding passed between the men. They knew Jace had found his mate. Jared took over the conversation to smooth over any awkwardness. "You haven't met Arie's brother yet, have you? He's a good bloke."

"I can meet him?"

"He's with Arie now," Kate said. "Why don't I take you?"

Anya clapped her hands and gave the brothers each a hug. "Spasibo, Jace. I will see you later."

As the women walked away, Hugh decided not to mince words. "This other woman is your mate?"

"She is." Jace felt instantly defensive, even though he'd grown up with these two and counted them as brothers. Realizing his back was up, Jace did his best to relax. "Her name is Edith. I'm afraid she's going to need more help than Arie and Anya combined."

Jared swore. "How long was she a prisoner?"

"Over a hundred years."

"Holy hell, Jace. How are you holding up?"

"It's not me I'm worried about."

"No, I suppose not," Hugh said. "Anything we can do, man. All you have to do is ask."

∞ ∞ ∞

ANYA WAITED IN THE HALLWAY while Kate knocked and called out softly. "Arie, it's Kate and Anya."

Emerson opened the door and ushered the two ladies inside. Anya ran to the bed where Arie still rested and threw her arms around her neck. "You look wonderful. I'm so happy."

"Anya, I'd like you to meet my brother, Aden."

Straightening from the hug, Anya turned to Aden and offered him a smile. "I'm so happy you have been reunited."

"Do you have any siblings?" Aden asked.

A spasm of pain crossed her face as her brother's image popped into her mind's eye. Her answer came out shorter than intended. "No."

Realizing his mistake, Aden looked helplessly at his sister. Arie took Anya's hand and squeezed. "I'm glad you got to come see me and meet everyone else. They've all been kind to you?"

"Oh, yes. I saw Jace, and he introduced me to Kate and Hugh and Jared. We also met Reya and her adorable malyshkas. I want to take them home with me so Edith can meet them."

"Let's focus on getting you healed first," Kate said. "And then hopefully Edith will feel more comfortable around additional people."

"Yes, good. I go back outside now so Arie can rest." Anya kissed Arie's cheek and gave Aden and Emerson a hug. "Make sure she sleeps."

"Scout's honor," Emerson said.

"What is a scout?"

"I'll explain it on our way down," Kate promised. Saying her goodbyes, she led Anya from the room. When they stepped back outside, Anya stiffened, her eyes wide. "Anya? What is it?"

"You don't feel that?" she asked, her voice barely above a whisper. She began to walk toward the tree line, moving as if in a trance. Kate followed, but Anya was past noticing.

She felt him. The man she could feel a world away. He was close. She had to find him.

Once in the trees, she picked up the pace. The earth directed Anya's feet with every step she took. Her stride quickened into a jog, then a run. Soon she moved like a blur through the trees, her enhanced eyesight taking in images and spitting them into her brain faster than she could process. She darted between trees and over fallen limbs and leaped over a stream without breaking stride. Her heart raced not from exertion but excitement. Her mystery man was so close she could taste it on the air.

Kate called out from behind, but she didn't care. Anya had to find him.

Breaking through the thick woods into a clearing, Anya stumbled to a halt. She'd lost the connection. The earth had lost the connection. Sitting abruptly on the ground, she closed her eyes and sent her thoughts winging through the earth and sky. *Where are you?*

No answer came. Anya wondered if it ever would.

Chapter 10

Samson and Lani stood together in the grassy area outside the bed-and-breakfast, watching little Nicola and Leia play with the other children. Since being reunited with her family, she'd spent every possible moment with her niece and nephew. The thought of going back to New Zealand—home—had excitement buzzing through her veins.

What is it?

Thinking of going home. I can't wait to show you everything I remember. It's been so long.

I'm excited, too. I've always wanted to travel.

Lani turned into his chest and stroked a hand along his jaw. *Nothing is better than being home with you.*

Anywhere you are, is home.

Her lips brushed against his. It was meant to be a tease, a promise of things to come. Samson's arms wrapped around her waist and took the kiss deeper, both forgetting for a moment they were in plain view of dozens of friends and family.

"Ew, gross!" said young Koko, making a gagging face with her little sister Kaiah. "Why do grownups do that?"

Laughing, Lani pulled away from Samson and knelt to Koko's level. "One day, you'll meet a boy you'll really like. When you're thirty years old or so. And I promise you'll want to do the same thing."

Her face scrunched up. "That's so old."

"Yes, I suppose it is," Lani said with her eyes twinkling. "I guess that makes me rather ancient."

"You don't look ancient. You're pretty."

Hugging the nine-year-old, Lani thanked her before standing again. "Go, have fun. It'll be time for lunch in just a bit."

As Koko ran off to join her sisters, Lani glanced over and spotted Kayne at the line of trees. He watched over the kids playing like a giant sentinel. Samson noticed and squeezed Lani's hand. *Go, talk to him.*

Nodding, Lani made her way over and stood beside the daemon in silence. Over the last few months, she'd gotten to know all the daemons that had stayed on the reservation. She genuinely liked them, respected them. She also knew Kayne well enough that he worried over something.

"You know, if I didn't know you had pure intentions, this would be a little creepy."

Kayne looked at her, startled. "What do you mean?"

"You're watching the little kids play. From the trees. Like a creeper."

Glancing around nervously, Kayne wondered if he should become invisible. The last thing he wanted was for Kateri or any of the other children to be frightened of him. When Lani began to laugh, he crossed his arms and glared at her. She didn't look nearly as terrified as he thought she should. "I fail to see what is so amusing."

"Oh, nothing. Look, Kateri is okay. She's surrounded by Elementals that would fight to the death to protect her and all the children. What is it that has you concerned?"

"She is mine to look after. The fact that she is so young does not change that fact, it only increases it."

"Okay, but that's not all. Talk to me."

He searched the surrounding area again. Instead of aloud, he used his special gift to communicate silently. *I fear there will be a daemon attack.*

Why? Did you see something?

No. But Balor has spies. He will know that we are gathered here, celebrating. It will anger him even further. I am only keeping a lookout.

What can we do? Should we set protection spells? Is there a way to block him or his spies?

I have done what I can, with Emrys' help.

Emrys had the most spell knowledge and power. There was a reason his name—and its English translation of Merlin—was synonymous with powerful sorcery. *Shouldn't I bring this up with the rest of the Elementals? So they can be on guard?*

Kayne sighed. She could hear it in her mind. *Not yet. I will be watching, for now. If need be, I can reach out to all at once.*

All? Really? She hadn't known he could do that.

It is not something I do often or lightly.

Looking up at him, Lani realized not for the first time that she had no idea the true extent of the daemons' power. *I'm still going to tell Samson. You know I can't hide this from him.*

I understand. Please, for now, keep it to yourselves.

I'll do it. For Jade.

Do not worry, Lani. Nothing will happen to anyone here, and nothing will ruin Jade and Talon's day.

Thank you. Leaving him to his silent guardianship, Lani rejoined Samson. "Want to go for a run? I'm feeling a little restless."

Samson understood that whatever she'd found out would have to wait until they were alone. Saying their goodbyes to Tristan and Reya, the couple headed to the woods. With Reya's help, Lani had converted Samson not long after the daemon attack on the reservation. They spent the long nights wrapped in each other's arms or practicing his new skills. Perhaps it was his teacher, but Lani thought Samson had progressed beautifully.

Hidden from view, they both shifted into air molecules before taking on the form of a wolf. Jade had asked them all not to scare the locals with panthers and leopards and other exotic animals wandering the Wisconsin woods, but no one would bat an eye at a wolf.

As they began their run, Lani told Samson about her conversation with Kayne. *He believes the daemons will attempt an attack.*

Shouldn't we warn the others?

He asked me not to. He doesn't want to cause a panic. They ran in silence for a while. Lani knew Samson didn't agree with Kayne's secretiveness; she didn't, either, but she did respect his knowledge on the matter. *We should practice your fighting skills.*

Samson's larger body brushed against hers, his head dipping low to nuzzle her shoulder as they ran. *You've taught me well.*

Yes, but there are so many other Elementals here. We could both learn something from them.

We could hold a sparring session. That's a good idea.

Of course it is. It was my idea.

Must be all that ancient wisdom. Samson yipped when Lani nipped at his flank in retaliation. He lowered and sprung forward in a playful pounce. Together they played, all notion of attack forgotten. Lani had had too few moments such as these. Only with Samson did she ever feel carefree.

Still, a part of her worried. She did her best not to dwell on the fact that Ferghus was still alive, plotting to bring her—and everyone she loved—to an end. Though she felt happier than she'd ever been, including her childhood, she still hated Ferghus for what he'd done.

Her best friend, Dezra, might still be out there, somewhere. Dezra had a brother, Dante, who had not been seen or heard from in decades. What if he had given in to the darkness from losing Dezra? Lani would never forgive herself.

She and Samson both had decided to be part of the group that would go to Ireland and find the entrance to Mag Mell. They would fight whatever daemons they had to in order to free others like Kayne and Emrys, and she prayed that they would also find Elemental hostages there.

She would do everything in her power to bring them home.

Chapter 11

Elan kicked at a rock, watching it bounce along the trail and into a pile of leaves, a plume of gold and red puffing out from the disturbance. He wanted to run in his wolf form, but that meant either arriving at his destination in the nude or carrying his clothes in his mouth. Neither sounded enjoyable at the moment.

Instead, he sauntered through the woods at a human pace. He'd promised Lenna that she could have the house to herself, but he hadn't thought through what he would actually occupy himself with while he was being such a good brother.

He wandered loosely in the direction of Black Bear Lake, where the former shadowmen from California were staying. He hadn't had direct contact with them but found himself curious about their situation. What would it be like to be saved from the brink of evil? Would a person be able to live with themselves? Ever find true happiness?

If he decided to undergo the transformation from Gifted to Elemental, would becoming a shadowman be in his future?

He and Lenna had spoken at length about being converted. It was obvious Lenna leaned that direction, since her mate—ugh, what a weird thing to think about—was a daemon with immortality. He didn't blame her one bit for wanting that future. She was safe from turning to the darkness.

But what of him? What if he didn't have a mate out there, now or even anytime soon? Talon had lived hundreds of years before meeting Jade. Same for Lani, with Samson, and her brother Tristan, with Reya.

Eternity was a long time. Having Lenna would be helpful, but at the moment, it was more than Elan really wanted to think about.

He wanted to have a beer and stare at a bonfire while making lewd jokes with other guys. Things that he should be doing at his age.

Breaking through the last of the thick woods, Elan's gaze scanned over the massive property that Talon had bought and cultivated. Several posh cabins lined the large lake, where canoes and kayaks waited for exploring. He spotted a group of shadowmen sparring in a clearing on the north side, while others played yard games and, sure enough, prepped wood for a giant fire.

It all seemed so...normal. Not at all what Elan had expected, but it was exactly what he needed.

The group closest to him raised hands in greeting. Approaching them first, Elan extended his hand and introduced himself. "Hey, I'm Elan Stone, from the Mescalero Tribe."

"Grey Elliot," the man with dark hair and eyes to match his name said first. "Need a drink?"

"Please."

"I'm Zane, Zane Mercer," said the next while Grey fished a beer from a cooler. Grey handed it to Elan, and he glanced at the label. Spotted Cow. Never heard of it.

"Jericho Winther," said the third before gesturing toward the bottle in Elan's hand. "It's good. Only sold in Wisconsin."

Taking a sip, Elan felt inclined to agree. "Are you all from California?"

"Most recently, yes," Zane replied with a flash of teeth, shoving his long braid from over his shoulder to his back. "You're one of the ones that can shift, aren't you?"

Grey groaned at his forwardness, but Elan didn't mind. He had questions of his own to ask. "I am. My sister and I both are."

"That's pretty incredible. Your whole tribe is Gifted, isn't it?"

"In more ways than one," answered a familiar voice. Elan looked up and grinned at Frances, who joined them with Emrys, one of the daemons who had been staying on the reservation. "Mind if we partake?"

Two more beers were passed out as the ones that had been stacking wood murmured an incantation to light the pile. Dusk had hit, the perfect time for fire and libations. A cheer went up as the flames caught and held, licking up the teepee of wood and sparking against the darkening sky.

The group that had been sparring decided to call it quits, joining the rest of the group in a drink as they watched the fire grow and swell. Emrys joined Elan as he found a seat on a log. "Where is your sister?"

Elan raised an eyebrow. "Where's Wynne?"

"Point taken. I am glad to see them trying to work things out. Both deserve happiness."

"Yeah," Elan answered, clearly not happy about the situation.

"What is it that bothers you? That your sister has a mate, or that her mate is a daemon?"

"Not really either of those. More that I feel like I'm losing her. That she's moving on without me. It's like we're Luke and Leia and Wynne's Han Solo, sweeping her away to the other side of the galaxy."

"Are these friends of yours?"

Elan stared at the daemon with absolute shock. "*Star Wars?* You've never heard of *Star Wars?*"

"I did not realize humans had advanced enough to wage war among the stars."

Elan choked out a laugh. Even Frances stifled a grin. "Dude, we've gotta get you caught up on pop culture. Please, let me be in charge of your education."

"I am all for it. I would very much like to pass as human, now that it seems we will be staying on earth for a while."

"Where should we start...do you have any favorite music?"

Emrys' brow furrowed. "Is Beethoven still popular?"

"Oh, boy. We've got our work cut out for us. We need some tunes ASAP. Anyone have a Bluetooth speaker handy?"

"On it," Grey replied, disappearing with preternatural speed and reappearing just moments later, speaker in hand. "Start him with the classics. Beatles and Elvis and work your way up."

Elan scrolled through the music on his phone and found what he wanted. Connecting to the speaker, he sat down and clinked his bottle against Emrys'. "You, my friend, are in for an auditory treat."

GERHARD HOLMES WATCHED THE FESTIVITIES from the shadows, an uncomfortable sense of longing filling his chest. He didn't know why he'd even bothered to come to this small town, where he knew he'd be forced into tight quarters with so many others.

He did know why. Jade. He owed her his life, for what little value remained. She had saved him, and he felt an inexplicable tie to her, as he knew the others felt for either her or her cousin, Kate.

Kate and Hugh had been good to them, as had Jade and Talon. The property Gerhard and the rest of the former shadowmen stayed was Talon's, after all. He let them live there while they made the reintroduction to polite society. Everyone else seemed to be doing fine with the arrangement.

Gerhard worried something was wrong with him. Even though Jade had helped to eradicate the darkness from his life, he feared it was only a temporary solution. A Band-Aid slapped over a gushing head wound, never quite enough to stem blood flow.

Still, he did his best to stay on the straight and narrow. He did his best to fit in. But even now, watching from the shadows, he longed to be a part of something he didn't think he ever truly could.

Gerhard sensed the other presence long before he spoke. "I'm heading to the fire, want to join?"

"No."

The other man paused at the rough tone. "Everything all right?"

"Has it ever been?"

"I don't think we've met. I'm Jace." Gerhard stared at the extended hand until Jace retracted. Trying again, Jace asked, "What's your name?"

"What does it matter? I'm leaving after tonight. It was a mistake to come here."

Jace studied the man with wild brown hair and thick eyebrows that seemed to be in a constant furrow over hazel eyes. His healer's heart reached out to the man who was obviously in a bad state. "Why do you think that?"

"I don't belong with you people."

Nodding, Jace watched the firelight, the men surrounding the area sipping beer and sharing stories. Music blared from a small speaker. Elvis. To the outside observer, it looked like a group of carefree friends on holiday. Jace knew better. He knew the man beside him knew better. "You see that man, there? His name is Frances. He influenced a human's mind to the point that the human held two women hostage and nearly killed one when he shot her. You know who that woman was?"

Jace had Gerhard's attention. "Who?"

"Jade. She almost died. Would have if Talon hadn't converted her. And you know what she did the next time she saw Frances?"

"She saved him."

"That's right. He was the first shadowman to have his soul restored. If Jade can forgive him for what he did, don't you think you could be redeemed, too?" Jace let the statement sit there for a few moments. "I'm going to grab a beer. Want to join me?"

After another hesitation, Gerhard began to move forward. "It's Gerhard."

"Nice to meet you. Ever had Spotted Cow before?"

Gerhard joined the others, though he still stood back. One baby step at a time. Jace stood with him, easily holding other conversations and seamlessly including Gerhard when he could. When he was halfway through his second drink, Gerhard felt himself begin to relax. He could do this. He could stand with a group of other men and enjoy a drink or two.

A soothing light slipped into his mind. It was so beautiful he felt ashamed to be sharing the same space. His knee hit the ground as he pressed his palms to his temples, crying out in pain.

Jace knelt before him instantly, opening himself up to investigate the cause of such sudden agony. Gerhard's head whipped up; his eyes lit with anger. "Don't."

Not one to frighten easy, Jace held both hands up to show he'd back off. "It's all right. I'm a healer; I can help."

"You can't help this."

Get out of my head.

If you would answer me, I wouldn't have to intrude.

The voice flowed through his body like sweet wine. The blood buzzed in his veins, and he felt a little bit woozy. *This is no place for you.*

I go where I want. He growled; the woman who'd invaded his mind and body simply laughed. *I do not scare so easy. We are connected. I know you have felt it. I come to you, and we talk.*

Don't you dare.

Fine. Not tonight. But you cannot hide from me.

She pulled away, and Gerhard felt instantly bereft. Her bright light had chased away shadows that had always been. With her gone, he felt more dangerous than ever.

"Gerhard? What's happened?"

"Nothing," he said with a hiss. "It's fine."

Standing, he marched back to his room. He couldn't be trusted around others. He didn't know what he'd do.

Jace watched him go, vowing that he would check on the man later. Gerhard needed friends now more than ever.

Chapter 12

After kicking her brother out of the house, Lenna showered and stood in a towel in her room, deciding between a casual jeans look or something dressier. It shouldn't have mattered since they planned on running in animal form and would have to remove said clothes, yet she couldn't seem to make a decision. "Okay, stop being stupid. He doesn't care what you wear. Don't be such a girl."

Besides, she really only had the one dress that she planned to wear to the wedding. Pulling on her favorite jeans with a teal and red patterned peasant blouse, Lenna ran a brush through her hair and left it down to air dry.

If Wynne wanted a girly girl, he would have to go find another mate.

Still, she felt nervous as she paced the house and checked on the food. She went for a dish she never screwed up—lasagna—and she'd found some freshly made French bread to serve with. Dinner first, then a run. Or would it be better to run first, work up an appetite?

Thinking about Wynne taking his clothes off to shift into wolf form built up a whole other kind of hunger.

They should cancel the run altogether. She was already pushing her self-control just by being in an enclosed space with him.

She sat down on the kitchen floor, elbows against her knees and forehead against her palms. She thought she could do this, be Wynne's mate, but she couldn't. She wasn't brave enough, tough enough. It was too much pressure, too much change.

Soothing hands rested against her forearms, sliding from elbow to wrist in an effort to calm her. She should have jumped or screamed at the presence of another, yet somehow, she'd known Wynne was there. The connection between them only grew with time.

"Lenna, grādh, look at me. Please. Tell me what is wrong."

Her hands shook, and she refused to look up. Looking at Wynne only muddled her brain. She needed to think clearly. *I can't. If I look at you, my brain turns mushy.*

Though he kept a straight face, Lenna could hear the amusement in his voice. Wynne settled on the ground beside her instead of forcing her to stand. *All right. Talk to me this way.*

Lenna felt awful for having to go through this again. She'd already talked out her feelings with Elan and thought that had been enough. Clearly, she'd been mistaken. *I'm nervous and a little terrified. Being around you makes me feel things. Things I've never felt before.*

I feel things for you I did not know were possible. I find myself nervous and a little terrified, as well.

His words calmed her. Knowing Wynne was experiencing the same things as she was helped more than anything else had. *Really?*

Yes. For our kind, there is only one other soul that matches ours. I have never felt so deeply for another.

What about...physical feelings?

I have those as well, but I would never push you farther than you are willing or able to go.

Lenna took a deep breath, let it out. Opened her eyes and lifted her head. Found those deep pools she could so easily drown in. "I've been standoffish because I felt like I would lose myself when I committed to you. Elan helped me see that wouldn't happen."

"I would not allow it. I enjoy every facet of you too much."

Lenna studied Wynne for a long time. A strange, electrical sensation sparked through her chest and tightened her belly. She felt light-headed and rooted to the ground, all at the same time.

Lust and something that could only be the beginnings of love washed over and through her.

"Oh, screw it." Grabbing his face between her palms, Lenna pulled his lips to hers and feasted.

If the move surprised Wynne, it took him only moments to recover. His palms cupped her cheeks as she knelt up and swung a leg over his lap. She pressed closer against his chest, allowing a baser instinct to take over. Her wolf hovered close to the surface, rising up to claim her mate. No wonder Lenna had been feeling such wild swings of emotion. She had been fighting herself, on a level few others could possibly understand.

Her wolf had been ready and willing to accept Wynne since the moment they met. Her animal had been able to cut out the human bullshit and see the truth.

Wynne was her mate, and they belonged together. Mind, soul, and body.

Lenna lifted her shirt over her head and let it drop to the floor. Wynne sucked in a breath, but Lenna's mouth was back on his, whatever dam that had been holding her back suddenly shattered. A passion she hadn't even known she possessed had been unleashed. Her fingers slipped down and found the hem of his shirt and brought it up, ripping it in her impatience.

Their kiss broke for a moment as the shirt cleared, and then his mouth found her chest, spreading fire wherever he touched.

She held him tight against her, sinking her fingers into his hair and letting out a gasp of breath.

Suddenly, her months of indecision seemed ridiculous. What had she waited for? She wanted Wynne, and he wanted her. They were mates, meant to be together. One hand released its grip on his hair and undid the button of her jeans. She was beyond reason, beyond thought. She only wanted to feel.

"Wait," Wynne said, but she distracted him with more kisses. His hands roamed her back and gripped her waist before moving to cup her face, forcing them apart. "Just a moment. Please. I want our first time to be memorable."

"Oh, it will be," Lenna said, moving in for another lip lock. She was done with talking.

Realizing he fought a losing battle, Wynne simply held onto her hips and stood up, taking it upon himself to find a bed. They raced up the stairs, though Lenna couldn't even tell they'd moved. She was too focused on the shape and feel of his bare chest.

Her back pressed into the bed, and she wrapped her legs around his waist, securing him tightly against her. She didn't want to lose contact for a second. She might lose her nerve if they did.

Wynne snapped her jeans off while his lips wandered her soft skin. His own pants followed and then they were skin to skin, veins sizzling with electricity, and every touch lighting a flame. He tried to go slow, to ensure her pleasure above all else, but Lenna had other ideas. She guided him to her entrance and arched back as he joined them together, the pleasure-pain the most intense feeling she'd ever experienced.

She let him take the lead, but when he continued to go slow for fear of hurting her, Lenna bucked and rolled until she had Wynne flat on his back. His eyes were wide with surprise and dark with lust. She loved looking at him like this. Such a powerful being under her complete control.

She began to move, allowing that same animal instinct to take over. All fear and doubt flew out the window. His hands gripped her hips with bruising force, and it only fueled the blazing fire sweeping through her. Lenna brought them both to the brink, hovering there for a suspended moment of time. Her eyes met his, joy and wonder passing between them before their hands linked and they took the plunge together.

They lay in silence for several minutes as their bodies cooled. Eyes closed, Lenna took a deep breath and let out a contented sigh. She'd collapsed against Wynne's hard chest and hadn't bothered to move. He didn't seem to mind.

His hands smoothed over her back, a soft caress that sent wonderful little shivers down her spine. If they never moved again, Lenna would be perfectly happy. Her stomach had other ideas. At the loud rumble, she giggled and looked up shyly. "Guess I worked up an appetite."

Wynne's gaze darkened; she loved it when he looked at her like that. "I believe I will always be hungry for you."

Her breath caught, hunger forgotten. Until she smelled the first tinge of something burning. Leaping to her feet, eyes wide, she swore and snatched a robe to wrap around her nude form. "The lasagna!"

Racing down the stairs, she grabbed hot pads and pulled the almost ruined dinner from the oven. The edges were slightly charred but otherwise seemed to be in good shape. Setting it on the stovetop, Lenna took the loaf of bread from its bag and stuck that in the oven to warm up. Only then did she face Wynne with a sheepish expression. "I've never messed up lasagna before."

"It looks perfectly edible," he replied, wrapping his arms around her waist. "Thank you for making dinner for me."

"Don't get used to it. This is all I know how to make."

He pulled back to look at her, humor in his eyes. "It is a good start."

Once the bread had warmed, Lenna took out butter and plates and served up hearty portions for both of them. Instead of sitting at the table, Lenna sat cross-legged on the living room floor in front of the fireplace. She looked at Wynne and gestured toward the dormant logs. "Can you—you know?" With a smirk, he flicked his fingers and sent a spark into the hearth. The flame caught and held as he settled on the floor beside her. "Seriously, so cool."

"You could have that ability."

Lenna looked up, her stomach knotting. Ready or not, here came that conversation. "You mean being converted to an Elemental? I've thought about it."

"What has you hesitating?"

She shrugged. "This whole concept is still pretty new. What about my family? Would I really want to outlive them? What if my brother decides not to convert? Then there's you."

"What do you mean?"

"Well, we're mates, right? How would that work, exactly?"

"I am not sure I get your meaning."

"Are we…compatible?"

He raised his eyebrows. "I would say so."

Heat settled in her cheeks. "Obviously, like that we are. I meant—what about kids and stuff? You're a daemon; I'm a human, Gifted or not. If I stayed this way, could we have a family? You know, one day, in the distant, distant future?"

"Lenna. Grādh. If at some point you would like children, even if I am not able to give that gift to you, we will figure out a way."

"Have you ever heard of a daemon and a human being mates? Having a family?"

"No, but then daemons and humans rarely interacted before this. Balor had us all under such a tight rule that a relationship such as this would not have been possible."

"What about daemons and Elementals?"

"Same answer. But we have to believe that the universe would not have matched us together if it were not meant to be." Taking her hand, he waited until she looked directly at him. "We must have faith."

At that moment, Lenna would have believed anything Wynne said. "What if you converted me?"

Shocked silence settled over them. Wynne sat back, though he retained his grip on her fingers. Lenna's heart pounded, awaiting his answer. "I—well, I had not thought of that. I have no idea what would happen if we attempted such a thing."

"You mean whether I would turn into a daemon or an Elemental, or if I would survive at all?"

"If there is even the slightest chance that you could be harmed, we absolutely will not try."

Lenna took a deep breath and let it out. They were certainly forging new paths here. "I have made one decision about our future."

"What is that?"

"I'm going with you to Ireland."

He wanted to say no. Lenna could see it written all over his face. If he tried, she would show him just how stubborn a Stone could be. And if he persisted, she would sneak onto the flight without his knowledge.

Her thoughts must have been as clear as his own, for he finally capitulated. "I should not have expected anything less from my fierce mate."

Ducking her head at his praise, Lenna tore off a chunk of bread and sopped up extra sauce before shoving it in her mouth. There was something else she wanted to talk about, but she didn't know how to bring it up.

She should have known Wynne would be able to see that, too. "What is it?"

"Earlier," she began, swallowing the last of her bite before continuing, "when I...took control. I'm not really sure what that was. I don't think it was all me."

"I was there. It was all you."

Huffing out a laugh, Lenna shook her head and tried to explain. "No, I mean, I think my wolf took over. In the kitchen and then again in the bedroom. I'm not normally quite so forward."

"I should hope not," Wynne said, baring his teeth. It only made Lenna laugh.

"You know what I mean. This is all new to me, but it was like as soon as I made the decision, my wolf was there to pounce." Literally.

"You have a very interesting relationship with your wolf. It is different than Elementals or even Gifted who have been converted. It is like your wolf is not just a physical manifestation, but that she has her own personality. Are you able to speak with her?"

Lenna tipped her head, truly thinking about it for the first time. "Yes. I can. I hadn't thought about it in quite that way before because she's always been there. It felt natural."

"Is it the same for the rest of your family and the other shifters?"

"I would imagine so, but we'd have to ask. Do you think that could affect a conversion? Would my wolf be okay?"

Wynne took the last bite of his lasagna as he thought through his answer. "She is a part of you, and you, her. I have to imagine she would convert right along with you."

"But?"

"But I do not have a solid answer. Our situation is particularly unique."

Picking the last of her bread apart, Lenna looked at the floor as she voiced her next thought. "If you were to convert me and I was to become like you, I'd be okay with that."

Setting his plate down, he moved Lenna's from her hand and pulled her into his lap instead. "I am happy to hear it. But we will not make any decisions tonight, or until we know more facts. Perhaps it is a good thing you will be coming to Ireland. If we are able to find answers anywhere, it will be there—or in Mag Mell."

"Would you...would you show me your horns?" Lenna asked, pointing to the crown of his head. "I want to see all of you. The real you."

Though he looked nervous, Wynne complied. Much like an Elemental when shifting, the air thickened and shimmered as the elegant horns grew from his forehead and extended into long, curved points. Lenna held her breath as she watched it happen, then reached up to brush her fingers gently along their smooth length. If Wynne had been expecting fear or loathing, all he received was rapt fascination.

"They're beautiful," Lenna said softly. Locking her gaze to his, she added, "You're beautiful."

Their lips met, and as they shifted from sitting to laying, all worries of the future were forgotten.

Chapter 13

Just before three o'clock in the morning, Elementals, Gifted, and daemons gathered in Talon and Jade's backyard. Word had spread about a training session, and it seemed everyone was eager to participate.

Kate spotted Arie arriving with Emerson, looking both stronger and lighter than the last time Kate had seen her. "Arie, I'm so happy to see you here. How are you feeling?"

"Much better, thank you." The fierce blonde stood tall, though Kate could still see some trepidation in her eyes. Emerson stood at her side, hands loose and gaze sharp. They weren't overly showy in their relationship, like other mates, but they moved with such coordinated unison it was easy to see that they were one unit. Every time one moved the other would make subtle adjustments. Always on guard. Kate had never seen two people so in tune with the other.

"That's wonderful news. Lani and Samson came up with the idea to hold a sparring session."

Aurelia's eyes never seemed to remain still. They continuously roved over her surroundings, gauging threats and processing every little detail. "I imagine each of us has wisdom to impart. It's still strange for me, to work with shadowmen instead of against them."

"Former shadowmen," Kate corrected gently. "I can understand your hesitation, but you can take it from me. I've been living with the majority of the group for several months, and I've found them to be the most courteous and thoughtful men I've ever met."

"You were speaking of me?" Hugh asked, joining his mate and sliding his hand around her waist. "Courteous and thoughtful?"

Kate slapped him playfully on his arm. "You've got a big enough ego as it is. Arie, I was hoping you would go over some things with me—well, a group of us. A lot of our women are not exactly fighters, but we would like to be able to defend ourselves if needed. Would you be willing to help?"

I hate to think of you in a combat situation.

It's not like I'm jumping at the chance, but we have to be realistic. We face a large threat, and you might not always be there to save the day.

Batman does not fail.

Sometimes he does, when he's got women on his mind.

Only one woman is on my mind.

Kate smiled lovingly at Hugh before facing Arie again. "So, what do you say?"

"I would love to help. I've been doing daily trainings with our little group. It's important that everyone can defend themselves, though I haven't dealt with daemons. For that, I was hoping to train myself."

"Kayne, Emrys, Wynne, and Irvyn have all been more than willing on that end. I want you to be at full strength before you do anything too strenuous. I'm sure Reya will agree."

Hearing her name, the healer joined the group. "What do I agree to?"

"Arie taking it easy until she's fully healed," Kate said.

"I agree," Emerson said, with a simultaneous "I'm fine," from Arie.

Stifling a chuckle, Kate gestured for Lani, Jade, and several other women to join them. Emerson and Hugh went to observe the daemon instruction while Arie scouted for an area large enough. When she was satisfied with the spot, Arie put her hands on her hips and studied each face before her. "I don't know you all, so why don't we start with introductions? Include your name and what abilities you have so I have an idea what to cover."

Kate went first, followed by Lani. "I'm able to communicate with animals or Elementals in animal form."

"Have you ever coordinated an attack with animals?"

"Only in extreme cases," Lani answered. "I don't like putting them in danger."

Though Kate could see Arie didn't necessarily agree, she continued without pause. "How are you with spells?"

"Getting better. Once my earlier memories were restored, the things I learned from Ferghus have come back. Frances was also teaching me while we traveled together."

Reese must have filled Arie in on some of the stories, for she took Lani's words in stride and moved on to the next.

Lenna, Nova, and Tala were all present, each able to shift into their animal form at will. Arie studied them for a moment before asking, "Have you ever tried other forms? Or partial shifting?"

The three women looked at each other before shaking their heads. Lenna answered for them. "No, though Wynne and I were talking last night"—a blush crept up her neck as she glanced quickly at the daemon and away again—"and he brought up an interesting theory. He believes my wolf is her own separate entity—different than an Elemental shifting."

Nova's eyebrow wrinkled as she thought that through. "Interesting. Might be true. Also, we're going to talk about that blush later."

Lenna turned a deeper shade of red. "What do you mean?"

The twins shared a grin. "Oh, yeah. We're going to talk."

"Much as I love to gossip," Aurelia said drily, "let's focus on fighting. You three, I want you to practice shifting one body part at a time. A hand into a paw, growing your muzzle to be able to bite. It will help if you need to fight in human form, and it will also help you have more control over your shifting. The rest of you, we're going to start with some easy spells. Jade, are there any trees here you're particularly fond of?"

"Nope, have at it," Jade said with a bit too gleeful grin.

"We're starting with fireballs. Let's try not to burn down the woods."

∞ ∞ ∞

SINKING INTO THE GRASS, KATE laid back to catch her breath. She couldn't remember feeling so physically tired since she'd been converted. Arie was something of a drill sergeant, but she was also a great instructor.

After fireballs had singed one too many tree limbs, Arie had performed a healing. She'd had the entire group join in, even the Gifted who hadn't done anything of the like before. Kate had never felt so much positive power concentrated in one area. Arie and Lani both had a natural affinity to the earth, and through them, the rest of the women were able to feel the same connection.

It had been a powerful, eye-opening moment. Kate felt more in tune with her own power than she ever had before.

Using that momentum, Arie had the Elementals practicing calling to the earth. They'd partnered off, facing off across several feet. Jade made faces at Kate as she knelt to the ground and formed a vine with her mind. When it slowly but surely made its way through the ground, Kate wrapped it around Jade's ankle before releasing it.

On Jade's turn, the vine rose so fast it took Kate off guard and she ended up with her butt on the ground. "Hey!"

"Sorry, sorry! Are you okay?"

"Nothing hurt but my pride."

Arie eyed Jade thoughtfully. "Are you certain you don't have an affinity to the earth?"

"Never have before," Jade said. "Maybe I'm just improving."

Arie grunted a response before kneeling to help Reya. After that, Arie had them practice both the fireballs and vines with moving targets. Kate had found herself on her butt several more times.

Now, she lay back and watched as the sun made its appearance in the eastern sky. Jade passed around bottles of water before joining Kate in the grass. "Who knew element manipulation could be so exhausting?"

"I would normally tell you to suck it up, but I do hope I haven't worn you out too much. You do still plan to examine Edith and Anya this morning?" Aurelia asked.

"Absolutely," Reya answered. "Just give us a few minutes."

"Five to ten, at most," Kate added.

"An hour. Maybe two," Jade said.

After a brief chuckle, Kate got to her feet and offered a helping hand first to Jade and then Reya. "Come on, ladies. We've got evil to eradicate."

Emerson, Dominic, Tristan, Talon, Jace, and Hugh left their group and joined the four women. Reese had volunteered to watch Nicola and Leia but would be keeping tabs through Dominic.

Kayne walked over and bowed his head respectfully. "We all volunteer to stand guard while you attempt this healing."

Aurelia stiffened, still uncomfortable around so many Elementals. Before she could respond, Emerson smoothed it over. "Thank you for the offer, but the women prefer their privacy for the time being."

"I understand. You have all trained with us now, and I am certain you will be able to put up an effective barrier. Just remember, guard above—and below."

Tristan shook Kayne's hand. "We will reach out if needed."

With that, the group left. Aurelia and Emerson took lead, using their preternatural speed to blur their movements. Traveling this way beat a car any day.

Do you need to feed? Hugh asked as they ran.

Yes. If it's anything like last time, I'm sure I will need to before and after.

Whatever my mate needs, I will provide.

Edith and Anya stayed in a secluded spot not far from Sun Valley. When the group slowed and approached the house at a human pace, Kate could see Anya's bob of brown hair as she peered at them through the window.

Kate, Reya, and Jade all fed from their mates before the men spread out in a wide circle to erect a barrier. The three women followed Arie inside, where they found Anya bouncing foot to foot. "You have come. Spasibo, spasibo. Come, meet Edith."

Kate saw Edith standing in the next room and instantly pictured her greeting guests in a mansion wearing a corset and billowy skirts. Though a petite woman, Edith held herself with such graceful poise Kate immediately felt like a pauper being granted an audience with the queen.

"So nice to meet you," Reya said, greeting the long-haired beauty first. "I'm Reya, this is Jade, and this is Kate."

"Such a pleasure to meet you all. Please, come in."

Reya sat on the edge of a chair while Kate and Jade made themselves comfortable on the floor. Edith sat while Anya, still too excited, practically danced beside her. Reya smiled at the young woman. "We'll be examining you first, correct?"

Edith answered for her. "We thought it might be easier, as she's had less time under Maurice's influence."

"Would it be all right with both of you if Jace joined us?"

"Of course," Anya answered.

"Yes, that would be fine."

"The rest of the men will stay outside as guards, unless we need them," Jade said. "Anya, do you feel comfortable feeding from one of them?"

"Emerson and Dominic have both offered," Aurelia said.

"Oh, yes. They are my brothers."

"Before we begin, I want to explain to you both what it will mean when I connect with you," Jade said. "I will have access to all of your memories. It can be fairly intrusive, and I just wanted you to know that ahead of time."

Edith looked at Aurelia before straightening her spine. "I have a gift that is also extremely intrusive. When I make contact with another, I am able to read them and their memories. Through touch, I am also able to communicate telepathically."

"Edith has seen my life. It is not so good. You can see it, too. This will help, yes?" Anya asked.

"Yes."

"Then I am ready."

"Where would you feel most comfortable?" Reya asked as Jace walked in. His eyes softened on seeing Edith, but he kept his distance.

"I will use the couch, if there is enough room for everyone."

Kate stood, closing her eyes for a moment to concentrate. Hugh could feel her anxiety. *You can do this. I am right here when you need me.*

I love you. "Right, as a warning to everyone, there is usually a strong pulse when the soul is won. Brace yourselves."

After everyone nodded, Kate relaxed and opened herself up to her gift. When her lashes lifted, Anya glowed the prettiest shade of yellow. Her goodness shone through even with the black stains battling for supremacy. Kate faced the darkness head on. She'd done it once, she'd do it twice more.

And she would rise victorious.

Chapter 14

Edith watched three virtual strangers go to battle for Anya. Power nearly hummed in the room as all three women first closed their eyes to concentrate. Reya's went vacant, Kate's narrowed in determination, and Jade faced a reality no one else could see.

While these miracle workers were impressive, Edith had a difficult time tearing her gaze from Jace. He sat beside Reya, simultaneously lending her strength and assisting in clearing Anya's blood of Maurice's taint. Ten minutes passed. Twenty. Sweat dripped from Kate's forehead. She was the only one speaking into the otherwise silent room, attempting to coax Anya's soul from hiding. To overcome the darkness and fight.

Kate let out a strangled breath as the power in the room surged, causing lights to flicker and crack. Edith braced for the shockwave, losing her breath in the process. One man materialized in time to catch Kate, while another did the same for Jade. Jace and Reya were pushed against the back of the chairs they occupied, and were unharmed, though Aurelia checked on them both before moving back to Anya's side.

Kate turned into her mate's embrace, and he moved them into a corner of the room. After she fed, she turned and nodded at Edith and Aurelia. "Her soul is won."

"Nice to meet you," Hugh said. "I'm Kate's mate, Hugh."

"Lovely to meet you, as well. I am Edith."

"And I'm Talon."

"You are both very strong men, to allow your women to put themselves at risk this way."

"Good thing Jade can't hear you," Kate said with a smile. "She'd go on a feminist rant."

"I apologize. I did not mean that women cannot make their own decisions. In my time, that was the way of the world."

"No offense taken. It does take a strong man to handle such stunningly beautiful, amazingly talented women," Kate replied, winking at her mate. "That's why I call him Batman."

"I am afraid I am unfamiliar with a man who is also a bat."

"Oh, don't worry. We'll make sure to catch you up."

"Her soul is really safe?" Aurelia asked.

"Yes. Now it's up to Jade and then the healers. This part takes some time."

"I would like to stay with Jade, if that will be all right with you," Talon said, directing this toward Edith.

She glanced between all the strangers in the room, obviously uncomfortable but willing to do whatever it took for Anya to heal. "Yes, that will be fine."

"We'll step outside," Kate said. "I could use some fresh air."

Aurelia sent Kate a grateful smile before murmuring encouragement to Anya. Several more minutes went by. Edith watched Jace, the strain clearly visible on his face. "Is it always like this?"

Talon answered. "Arie was the first they attempted this kind of healing on. With Jade, the first few shadowmen she connected with physically knocked her out. It was terrifying. Since then, she's able to keep conscious, but she needs recovery time."

Tears began to flow down Jade's cheeks. Edith understood, her heart reaching out to the women who had to relive Anya's memories. She had done the same when she first met Anya. She hoped, after this, that Anya would be able to separate herself from her past. Doing so would help her live a full and happy life.

Jade's eyes popped open wide before she sank straight to the ground. Prepared for that eventuality, Talon cradled her in his arms like a baby. It only took a few moments before she blinked him into focus. Jade turned to look at Edith and Aurelia, nodding to let them know it was done.

"Excuse us," Talon said politely before carrying his fiancée outside to recover.

It was down to Reya and Jace. Edith wished there was some way she could help. Lend him her strength. She knew Tristan did so for Reya even from outside. Jace had no one.

Not true. He had her. Edith might not be ready for their relationship, but she was no coward.

Closing her eyes, she took a few deep, settling breaths. When she opened her connection to Jace, mind-numbing pain hit her full force and settled in her limbs as if she'd been drugged. She cried out with the pain of it but refused to back down. Maurice would not win this battle or any other.

Forcing her way through the dark and utter agony, Edith found the bright spot that was Jace. His soul, laid bare before her. He was so beautiful, so serene. A bright, searing light that healed wherever it touched.

I am here, she said softly. *Take what you need.*

You shouldn't be here. It's not safe for you.

I am your mate and I will do what is necessary to secure your health and safety.

Her tone brooked no argument. He knew well enough not to try. Instead, he borrowed her strength and forged ahead. Even with the short amount of time Anya had been converted, Maurice's influence had sunk deep. This was no easy task.

I believe in you, came Edith's voice, a breath of fresh air. *We will not let Maurice control us or those we love. We will win. We will rise victorious.*

Reya and Jace came back into their own bodies with a gasp. Tristan was there, hugging his mate to his chest. Jace's gaze met Edith's with wonder and something deeper. Something she dared not name.

"Thank you," he said, floored by her complete selflessness.

She nodded once in acknowledgment before moving to Anya's side. The fact that she trembled didn't go unnoticed by Jace. Anya's long lashes lifted, her own tears drying against her cheeks. "Edith? Arie?"

"We're here," Aurelia said, squeezing one hand while Edith grasped the other. "How do you feel?"

"Tired, but good. It is done?"

"Yes, sweetie. It's all done."

"Okay. I sleep now."

Chuckling, Aurelia helped Anya to her feet and led her to the bedroom. Alone with Jace, Edith turned toward him and looked everywhere but at his face. "You need to feed."

"I will."

Her eyes met his for just a moment before dancing away again. "Can I get you something? A drink that is not blood? Something to eat?"

"No, thank you."

"Okay. Well." Edith clasped her hands, pressed her thumbs together. When Jace stood to leave, she murmured an exclamation before closing the distance between them and wrapping her arms around his waist. "I am so glad you are well."

Before she could talk herself out of it, she lifted herself on tippy-toe and kissed his cheek. A spark of electricity traveled from the point of contact and through each of their bloodstreams to settle as butterflies in their stomachs. She looked at him in shock as Aurelia came back into the room.

"Anya's resting."

"Good. That is good."

"Yes. Very good." Jace lingered another moment before gesturing outside. "I'll be right back."

"What's going on there?" Aurelia asked, not expecting an answer.

"I kissed him," Edith blurted out. At Aurelia's shocked look, she quickly added, "On the cheek."

"Well, look at you, Miss Floozy."

Edith straightened with indignation. "I am no such thing."

"Of course not. You feel attraction for your mate. It's perfectly natural."

"You feel this? All the time?"

"Edith." Aurelia approached the woman who had gotten her through the worst times of her life. "I promise you, it will all be fine. You know how terrified I was of being intimate with Emerson, but he is my perfect match in every way, as I believe Jace is for you. When you're ready, I know Jace will do everything in his power to make you feel safe and loved."

She let out a breath and nodded. "I know. I know he will."

Jade returned, looking refreshed after feeding from Talon. "Ready for round two?"

"Has everyone recovered?" Edith asked.

"Don't worry," Jade said and, without thinking, placed her palm against Edith's arm. A surge of power exploded out and sent each into the other's memories.

Tumbling down a long, dark tunnel, Jade attempted to catch her balance but couldn't tell which way was up, which way was down. She had been sent spinning at a dizzying speed, no control over her direction or orientation.

She felt another presence in the darkness. Evil. Terrifying. Mocking laughter floated just outside her peripherals, long fingers brushing against her skin. She cringed against the contact, curling into a ball in an attempt to save herself from the torture.

Jade searched the darkness for any spark of light, of hope. None could be found. She recognized Maurice's voice by now. Could smell his rank stench. She knew what was coming for her. What was coming for all of them.

She didn't want him to touch her. Each time he did, she would see his memories. Every single vile act he'd ever done. Every woman he'd hurt or raped. Every body he'd drained of blood and left for dead. The small slice of exhilaration he mistook for real pleasure.

Jade lay still and accepted what was to come. There was no other choice for her. No other choice...

"Jade!"

Ripped from the darkness, Jade opened her eyes and gasped for breath. She expelled evil as one would water from the lungs. Heaving and retching up bile, Jade took sobbing breaths as she attempted to reconcile where she had just been with reality.

Campfires and evergreens. Talon.

Curling into a ball, she allowed her mate to stroke a hand over her hair, her back. He soothed even when he felt his heart had been lodged in his throat.

"What the hell just happened?" he asked with venom in his tone.

Edith rocked on the ground, tears flowing freely from her eyes. "I am sorry. I am so, so sorry."

Aurelia hugged Edith and tried to soothe. Jace appeared and pulled her into his lap, rocking her like a child. "What is it? What happened?"

"Jade...she got sucked in...we cannot do this. I cannot."

Jade finally lifted her head, her breath slowly returning to normal. "It's my fault."

"This is too dangerous," Talon began, but Jade waved him off.

"It's my fault. I touched her arm without thinking. Neither of us was ready."

"He is right," Edith said. "This is too dangerous. I will not allow you to do this."

"It'll be fine. I'll know what to expect."

"No." Rising to her feet, Edith steeled herself. "Thank you all for offering to help, but we cannot do this. I cannot. Please, all of you, leave. I will watch over Anya."

And before anyone could argue, Edith went to her room and closed the door behind.

Chapter 15

Pearl rearranged the flowers adorning the table for the third time. She'd kept the theme simple by using mason jars and wildflowers, but she still wanted the night to be perfect.

She was, after all, the reason Jade and Talon were even getting married. If it hadn't been for her help, those two never would have figured it out. It was bad enough that they'd waited so long after getting engaged and had refused an extravagant engagement party, agreeing only close family and a few friends could attend. Pearl had remained firm on the rehearsal dinner, even when she'd capitulated and allowed Jade to have her way with a lowkey barbecue instead of the fancy sit-down Pearl would have preferred.

Easy-going Pearl, that's what people liked to call her.

"How's this?" Micah called down from the roof, where he affixed string lights from a pole to achieve a gazebo effect.

"A little more to the left," Pearl said, stepping back to get a better view. Dozens of tables had been fitted with white tablecloths, and though it would be a buffet line of barbecue, each place setting still had a real plate and silverware. The jars of flowers were spaced evenly apart every two feet, with candles between.

Micah, Jack, and Rick had been at work on the light gazebo for the better part of an hour while caterers set up the food tables and more volunteers stuck tiki lights in the ground. The scent of chicken and beef filled the air as the chef she'd hired worked out of a mobile grilling station.

Micah had volunteered to cook, but Pearl didn't want him manning the grill all night. He was her date, after all.

When she'd approved the final string light, Micah climbed down and joined her side. "It all looks amazing, sweetheart. And it looks like the weather will hold."

"Of course it will." If it knew what was good for it. "Jack, Rick, thanks for your help. Go on home and get dressed, we'll see you in two hours."

"Why don't you get cleaned up, too? I think everything is ready."

"I will." She stood on tiptoe to kiss her husband's cheek. "Join me, won't you?"

When she pinched his side and he went to retaliate, Pearl took off for the house, her peal of laughter floating out behind.

∞ ∞ ∞

THE PHOTOGRAPHER ARRIVED HALF AN hour before the first guests. All seven kids were home from the neighbors and their outfits had passed Pearl's inspection. She stepped outside with Micah at her side and took one last look at their hard work. "It's like a fairy tale."

"Jade will love it. Now, promise me you'll enjoy yourself."

"Oh, I already have," she said with a laugh as Micah leaned down and laid a loud kiss on her lips. "But I promise."

"How many people are expected tonight?"

"Our family, Talon's family, and Jade insisted on all these friends from...wherever. I'm not sure who they all are. All in all, there will be a couple hundred."

"Good thing we have tomorrow to recover before the wedding on Sunday."

"Remember, we're having all the kids over tomorrow for a sleepover."

"Yes, but I'll be upstairs with noise-canceling headphones."

Pearl rolled her eyes but knew her husband was kidding. Mostly. "Sure thing, sweetie. Oh, I think our first guests are here. Let's go."

Her parents arrived first, followed closely by Emma and Amber with their families. Jade and Talon had been told to arrive half an hour later than everyone else, so they could make a grand entrance.

The extended family began trickling in. The compliments on the décor filled her heart with joy. When Kate arrived with her fiancé and a rather large group of extraordinarily good-looking men, Pearl found herself slightly tongue-tied. "Welcome to our home. I'm Pearl, Jade's favorite sister. I'd love to meet each of you before you find your seats."

Hugh and Jared both gave Pearl a hug, though she'd just met Jared the day before. She found the entire group of tall, bulky men had unfailing manners.

"Nice to meet you, I'm Frances Borg."

"And hello to you, Frances. Are you single?"

He choked out a laugh, unsure how to respond. Pearl simply raised an eyebrow as she waited. "Yes, ma'am."

"We'll see what we can do to change that. Mingle, and then have a seat wherever you'd like." The next man introduced himself, and though Pearl did her best to remember names, they quickly began to blur.

A man with dark hair and striking gray eyes bowed over her hand as she neared the end of the line. "Grey Elliot, ma'am."

"Elliot?"

"Yes, ma'am."

"Any relation to my husband, here?" she asked with a laugh.

Micah turned from his own conversation and shook Grey's hand. "Nice to meet you, I'm Micah. Micah Elliot."

"I must admit, I've lost contact with most of my family, but I suppose we shouldn't discount the possibility."

"Mama!" Aspen ran over, the eldest girl of the seven siblings. "Ashton threw a stick at me, and it had mud on it and now there's a spot on my dress!"

Pearl knelt to inspect the soiled dress while Grey stared, wide-eyed and chest tight. When he spoke, his voice came out barely above a whisper. "Vivienne?"

Having wiped the dirt off, Pearl stood as Aspen took off again. "What was that?"

Grey watched the little girl running toward the other children and nearly broke down. Shaking himself out of his momentary daze, he looked at Pearl with a softness that hadn't existed before. "She looks exactly like my sister."

"Perhaps we should have a beer while we chat," Micah suggested. "Where did you say you're from?"

Bewildered by the strange turn of events, Pearl watched the two men for a moment before turning back to her guests. She still had a line to get through, and Jade would be arriving any minute.

Talon's family arrived next, along with four men who easily reached over seven feet tall. Something about them made Pearl nervous, though she couldn't put her finger on what it was. Then she noticed Lenna held the hand of one and took a closer look. Were they brothers? What in the world did their parents look like? Their poor mom—Pearl could only imagine how big they had been as babies.

As she greeted each person, she noticed Valentina flicking nervous glances across the yard. Pearl looked that way, too, but there was so much of a crowd gathered she couldn't pinpoint the source of Valentina's nerves.

"Are you all right?" Pearl asked the younger woman.

Though Valentina nodded, Pearl wasn't convinced. "Yup. Fine. Totally. It's beautiful, Pearl. Nice job."

"Thanks. Enjoy!"

The last person joined the fray when Emma appeared from the front of the house. "Jade and Talon have arrived."

Pearl hurried to the front to greet them. Talon looked dapper as always in his black suit and vest, with no tie or jacket. Jade wore a floor-length black dress with a spattering of small rosebuds on the waterfall skirt and sheer sleeves that ended at the elbow with little bows. Pearl approved.

"Welcome, you two! You look wonderful. Come on back, everyone's waiting."

She brought them through the house so that they appeared on the second-floor deck, where they were met with cheers and applause. Jade and Talon both waved before making their way down the steps, hand in hand. As they greeted their guests, Pearl did her last-minute checks with the catering staff.

Pearl kept herself busy playing hostess, making sure her guests were fed and happy. After speeches and a champagne toast, she directed the men to light the bonfires.

With her duties done, Pearl sighed and relaxed into Micah's chest. The kids roasted marshmallows at the fire, each in varying degrees of exhaustion. She focused on Hazel and Perrin, who had formed an attachment to another set of twins, Leia and Nicola. There was something different about those two. Besides being beyond their years in motor and speech skills, they seemed to have an unusual connection.

Much like her own Hazel and Perrin.

Though she hadn't said as much to anyone else, even Micah, she'd noticed little things ever since the girls were born. How they seemed to know what the other was thinking. And, like the Amiri siblings, how they seemed miles above other children their age.

Pearl knew it wasn't just a mother's pride. There was something extra special about her babies. And though she hadn't called Jade out on it yet, she knew there was something more going on with her and Talon, not to mention the rest of the group they'd invited to the wedding.

The others in their family might be happy playing ignorant, but Pearl knew she would find out the whole truth eventually. Too many strange things had happened to call them coincidence. She might have happily remained in bliss with the rest of them, but she knew deep down that her youngest children were somehow involved in whatever was happening.

Jade couldn't evade her much longer. When Pearl put her mind to something, by God, it got done.

For tonight, she would enjoy the success of the party. Tomorrow was another day.

PEOPLE WATCHING HAD ALWAYS BEEN one of Reese's favorite activities. As a writer, she considered things like that and staring out windows to be work. Convincing Dominic of that fact wasn't always so easy.

Still, he liked to watch her watching others. Her deep brown eyes sparkled as she took in the beautifully decorated yard, the mixture of Jade's family with Elementals and daemons. Some of the looks Jade's family gave the hulking men made her giggle.

Arie and Emerson stood at the edge of the tables, keeping a sharp eye on the group. Reese was proud of Arie; she faced many fears coming to a social event such as this. It helped to have Emerson at her side and her brother—who walked toward them now, drinks in hand—to lean on.

Reese smoothed a hand over her baby bump, which grew daily. Jace had been keeping a close eye on their development, since they still didn't know how the conversion had affected the babies. Edith had told her they would be fine, and while she trusted the woman's opinion, she still worried.

"It's too bad Edith and Anya can't be here," Reese said. She'd stayed away from the healing session on Dominic's directive. He refused to put her in any situation that had the slightest possibility for danger. "They will try again with Edith, won't they?"

"It was her decision," Dominic said. "We will all help her to trust the women enough to try again. I know Reya, Kate, and Jade are willing."

"But they won't all be together much longer. Reya will be going back to New Zealand, Kate to California. She can't wait too long."

Dominic wrapped an arm around her waist, his palm against her stomach, fingers splayed. "It will all work out."

As he kissed her neck and Reese forgot all about Edith and Anya and even the spread of food that smelled so appetizing, an older woman approached, her eyes in a squint. "Who are you?"

"I'm Reese," she answered brightly. "This is Dominic. We're friends of Jade."

"Pregnant?"

Startled by the straightforwardness of the question, Reese nodded. "That's right."

"You two married?"

"Ah, well..."

"Yes, we are. Reese is my other half and I love her more than life itself."

The woman nodded with satisfaction. "Good. My niece waited too long, but she found a good man."

Pearl hurried over to intercept. "Aunt Maude, have you gotten some food yet?"

"No. What is this business about getting it myself? What do I look like, a waitress?"

"Of course not. Ashton here is happy to help." Pearl gestured for her eldest to come over. "Will you get Aunt Maude a plate of food?"

He nodded and helped the woman to a seat. She eyed him curiously. "Any girlfriends yet?"

Though he sent his mom a wide-eyed look, Ashton got Maude into a seat before running off to the buffet line. Reese chuckled as Pearl made apologies. "That's our great-Aunt Maude. She's from a different time."

"Oh, I love it. No worries." Squeezing Reese's arm, Pearl left to smooth over the next awkward situation. Reese leaned into Dominic with a grin. "So, married, are we?"

He cleared his throat. "It was just to appease her."

"She scared you a little, didn't she?"

"I have a healthy respect for my elders." Reese kept smiling at her mate; he looked at her with exasperation. "I realize we've never discussed marriage."

"Oh, Dominic. I'll put you out of your misery, even though you're adorable when you get all tongue-tied. I don't need a wedding. I've got no family to invite. If you want to make us legally official, we could go to the courthouse. You've already got me for life, and there's no backing out of that."

"We could still have a celebration. You do have a family now. Arie, Edith, Anya. Not to mention my brother, Arie's brother. Jace. And I'm sure Gabi and Jordan would love to be part of a wedding."

"Huh. I guess you're right. Still, we'll keep it small. Something in our yard, once we move back to Duluth?"

"Deal." Dominic kissed her deeply, and for a moment they both forgot where they were. Only the clinking of glasses alerted them to their surroundings.

A man stood and introduced himself as Jade's grandfather. "I just wanted to be the first to wish Jade and Talon a happy life together. Talon, you have proven yourself a man worthy of my granddaughter. I only wish my dear Naomi could be here with us, but I know she watches with a smile on her face."

Jade stood with Talon several feet away. Reese could see the tears glittering in Jade's eyes as Talon wrapped his arms around her. "I will leave you with just a few words of advice. Put each other first ninety percent of the time, and yourself the other ten percent. It's okay to go to bed angry, because you will always wake with a fresh perspective. And just remember, love is like a machine. Sometimes you just need a good screw to fix it."

Most of the family went wide-eyed as they choked out a forced chuckle. The rest of the crowd laughed, clapping as Jade's grandfather went over to kiss Jade on the cheek and shake Talon's hand. Jade's father stood next, followed by Viktor, the acknowledged leader of the Mescalero reservation and a stand-in for Talon's own parents.

Once speeches were done and large quantities of food had been consumed, Reese and Dominic joined Aurelia and Emerson as some of the men lit the waiting bonfires.

"Are you enjoying yourself?" Reese asked Aurelia.

"Surprisingly, yes. I rather like Jade's family."

"Her grandpa is a hoot, isn't he? We spoke with him for a bit, and he had me cracking up."

"Please, don't," Dominic began, but Reese barreled on through.

"What did the elephant say to the naked man?" When Aurelia shrugged, Reese answered, "How do you breathe through that tiny thing?"

She laughed as hard then as when she'd heard it. The rest chuckled to placate her. "Anyway, are you both planning on training in the morning again?"

"Yes," Aurelia said. "We might as well take advantage of the time we have together."

"I wish I could go, though I don't mind watching Reya's twins. Good practice and all that."

"You've come so far with our practices. We will continue once we settle, and I'll have new things to go over with you, Edith, and Anya."

Aurelia's expression changed, from hopeful to clouded. Reese understood. "She'll try again. We'll all make sure of it."

"I just—I want this for Edith."

"She does, too. But we have to remember she's been dealing with this for longer than any of us have been alive. I don't think she even remembers what it feels like to live without pain or fear. She just needs more time."

"We can give her that," Emerson said. "Dominic and I will head to his property tomorrow to meet with the contractors. Once they are settled in a permanent home, everything else will be easier."

"I'm so excited to go back." Reese placed both palms against her stomach, surprised. "Oh! I think the babies are excited, too."

Grabbing Dominic's hands, she placed them under hers. Tiny nudges rippled under their palms. Dominic's eyes grew wide. "Is that?"

"Yes. Our babies are kicking."

Aurelia stared at Reese's stomach for a moment before reaching out hesitantly. "Can I...?"

"Of course!" Reese grabbed her hand and guided it to the right spot. "Wait. There it is."

"Oh, wow," Aurelia murmured, her gaze switching to Reese's and then Emerson's. "That's amazing. I've never felt anything like it."

Emerson's hand joined Aurelia's, the four of them forming a protective circle for Reese's unborn children. Reese knew, in that moment, that Dominic had been right. She did have a family.

Chapter 16

Strings of lights draped from a harbor created soft, romantic lighting in the small clearing in the woods. Aurelia watched as Lani walked down the aisle, arm linked with Samson. Talon waited under a hand-carved trellis, a bright smile on his face.

When Jade appeared, the crowd stood with a collective sigh. Joy radiated from every single body present. Nothing could go wrong this night. Jade deserved all the happiness in the world.

Though they had only just met, Aurelia felt she knew Jade better than almost anyone. Because of the healing, Aurelia now had a deep, unbreakable connection to both Jade and Kate. They had shared her deepest, darkest memories. They'd gone to battle together for her very soul.

With the help of three miraculous women, Aurelia felt truly free from Maurice. His influence had been eradicated from every part of her. Anya, too. And soon, Edith.

Jade moved at a slow, steady pace, her gaze locked on her mate. Emerson's arm wrapped tighter around Aurelia's back, and she leaned into him, content.

Viktor and Malakai oversaw the procession, waiting for Jade to take Talon's hands before beginning. "Friends, family, we are gathered here to celebrate the love between Talon and Jade. This night, they will create an unbreakable bond. Tonight, they will become husband and wife."

Viktor took his turn, cupping Talon and Jade's clasped hands in his. "I would like to begin with a traditional Apache blessing."

The ground rumbled. The crowd adjusted their stances, attempting to keep their balance as great tremors shook and pulled at the earth. Those capable of fighting automatically began to form a protective circle around those unable.

Aurelia stood beside her mate and his brother, prepared for anything that may come. Around them, Elementals and the few Gifted that could shift did so with great speed. Daemons unleashed their horns and razor-sharp claws. Others, like Aurelia, crouched in their human form and waited.

I love you, woman.

You are my life.

With a great crack the ground split open. Aurelia winced, the earth's pain reverberating through her own chest. She knew

Emerson could feel it, too. She vowed to heal Mother Earth's wounds before this night was done.

With a hearty roar, daemons rose through the cracks and poured through the woods. The circle of Elementals braced for impact.

The first daemon struck the barrier and cried out in pain. One by one, they began to drop like flies struck by a bug zapper. Burns blistered flesh and singed hair.

Get ready, said a voice echoing through all Elemental and Gifted minds. *They will breach soon.*

Aurelia glanced over at Kayne, a truly frightening vision in all his daemon glory. If someone had told her even a few weeks ago she'd be fighting alongside daemons and former shadowmen, she'd have laughed in their face. Life could take some strange turns.

She could see several daemons working furiously at unraveling the protective spell. More hugged their wounds and glared; they hadn't expected to come up against such opposition. Balor had promised them an easy fight. To attack during the wedding so all fighters would be distracted and burdened with protecting the innocent.

Emrys and Frances struggled to keep the barrier intact. Kayne locked eyes with a daemon with golden eyes. He seemed to be the leader of the charge, and Aurelia realized he must be

Ferghus. When Emrys and Frances both grunted with pain, Kayne spoke to everyone again. *It's time.*

The first daemon broke through the barrier with a great roar. He snarled and moved to attack; three former shadowmen—Lucius, Silas, and Augustus—quickly dispatched him.

He might have been the first, but he wasn't the only.

With a clap of air that temporarily knocked the wind from Aurelia's lungs, the barrier dispersed, and Aurelia faced off with her first daemon. He charged forward with the favored weapon, a long spear. Slipping to the side of the sharp end, Aurelia moved in and delivered several quick blows before moving out of range. The daemon brought the weapon up and as it came barreling down, Aurelia put on a burst of speed and aimed for the daemon's throat. Sharp claws protruded from her fingertips as she ripped and pulled. The spear dropped to the ground. Without pausing, Aurelia scooped it up and met her next opponent on even ground.

Beside her, Emerson and Dominic fought three at once. Since they'd woken from their time in the earth, Aurelia had been building up her mental abilities while Emerson practiced variations of his own power. Instead of fully taking over control of a mind and unleashing incredible pain as he'd always done, Emerson shot out short bursts that temporarily disabled his opponent. Doing so took little concentration on his part and gave him a slight edge. Even a moment or two of hesitation on the daemon's end could be fatal.

Throughout the clearing Elementals and Gifted fought the intruders, using the techniques Kayne, Emrys, Wynne, and Irvyn had gone over for the last two mornings. She saw the Stone twins from the reservation working in tandem to take down a daemon, while Atienn, Chayton, Nova, and Tala watched each other's backs.

Talon, Samson, and Lani protected a small group of women as they used their own gifts to help. Jade and Kate, who tried to pinpoint any daemons that possessed Tuatha Dé Danann blood. Anya, who had refused to stay home, sat on the ground with her hands dug in the earth. Single shoots of vines would spring up to trip a daemon or grab at their hands. Like Emerson, Anya had trained for more practical attacks.

Aurelia parried a blow and from the corner of her eye, she saw a daemon slip through Anya's guards. Heart in her throat, Aurelia jabbed at the daemon she fought and spun to intercept. Before she could, a man—a former shadowman—beat her to it.

He had unruly hair the length of his shoulders and a pair of intense hazel eyes. Letting out a feral growl, he shredded the daemon like a lion would a gazelle. Only once the threat had been eradicated did he turn his penetrating gaze to Anya.

She stumbled back with a soft gasp. Aurelia had paused when he'd taken care of the immediate threat, but she began to move forward again at the thought that Anya might be in distress. Anya stared at the former shadowman with her wide, innocent eyes. "It's you."

The man who had decimated his opponent with such brutal force suddenly looked uneasy. Anya reached out, but he spun away.

Aurelia wanted to find out more, but she had more pressing matters.

Reya cast quick spells of fire while Tristan moved like a force of nature. Even in a group of excellent fighters, Aurelia found herself impressed at his speed and utter ruthlessness.

The former shadowmen fought as if they had a score to settle—and they did. Aurelia gave them a grudging respect, knowing the daemons had influenced their evil behavior. She got a second chance; she supposed they deserved one, as well.

The Elementals quickly gained the upper hand. Ferghus looked furious, his gaze darting between the traitor daemons and Lani. In her fighting, Aurelia had moved closer to the other woman, and on seeing how she'd grabbed Ferghus' attention, Aurelia crouched at Lani's side.

"I hear you like taking women," Aurelia said with a sneer. "Why don't you try that with me?"

Ferghus lunged. Aurelia went left as Lani went right. Both landed a strike to his ribs. He spun, furious. "You won't get away from me again, little flower. Your new friend can join you." He paused, seeming to have an amusing thought. "Come with me now, and I'll reunite you with your other little friend."

Lani faltered, for just a moment. Ferghus had managed to strike a low blow, but Aurelia didn't waste time. She threw her spear, aiming directly for the daemon's heart. She didn't believe it would hit its target; she just needed a distraction. As Ferghus moved to block the attack, Aurelia ran forward so fast she disappeared from view.

Ferghus looked directly at her. Time slowed. His hand rose, claws extended. Still on her forward trajectory, Aurelia couldn't do anything but move unerringly closer to the sharp points. She couldn't understand how he accomplished this, but one thing was clear to her in that moment; she had seriously underestimated the daemon's power.

A blur of motion moved in behind the daemon. His eyes widened in shock and his hands flew out toward his sides. Aurelia made contact simultaneously at solar plexus and gut with a two-handed punch. Ferghus flew back and Tristan appeared in his place.

"What the hell?" Aurelia asked, her question encompassing everything from Ferghus' time wielding to Tristan's sudden appearance.

"Later." Tristan spun, so that when Ferghus recovered he now faced two pissed off women and a phaser.

He snarled and let out an unearthly yell, causing all fighting to cease. The earth cracked open once again and all daemons, including the fallen, slipped through.

Emerson reached Aurelia just a moment later, wrapping his arms around her waist. He looked to Tristan with a respect he offered few. "Thank you."

They looked around, taking stock. Several were wounded, but none severely. Reya began healing what she could as those who had shifted began turning back to their human forms. Aurelia made a quick sweep for the man that had saved Anya, but he was nowhere to be found.

"Well," Jade said, speaking above the low murmurs, "that was quite the wedding rehearsal."

A low chuckle spread through the crowd, more from relief than amusement. Jared clapped his brother on the back as Reya healed a particularly deep gash on his forearm. "I can't believe that worked."

"Yes," Kayne said. "Well done, Tristan."

Lani had finally convinced Kayne to warn the others about a possible daemon threat that morning during a sparring practice. Tristan had come up with the idea of having a fake wedding to provoke the attack. He inclined his head in acknowledgment. "And to you, for your diligence. Is everyone else safe?"

Dominic spoke up. "Reese felt a disturbance from town, but she created a thunderstorm as cover. It seems the battle was contained in this area."

"She created a storm?" one of the former shadowmen asked.

Dominic smiled, his chest puffing out. "She is very talented."

"Why don't we all take a few, feed if needed, and round up any of those who were not able to join us? We still need to meet," Tristan said.

Talon spoke up. "I have enough blood at our home; all are welcome."

"We can hold the meeting there, as well. We'll start in an hour?" Jade said.

There were nods of agreement all around. Anya stood and looked at Aurelia. "I will heal the earth."

"Of course. I will help you."

"As will I," Lani offered.

"Do you need more help?" Tristan asked.

"Three will be enough. We are strong," Anya replied.

"Of that, I am absolutely certain. A few of us will stay to watch over you."

Tristan, Emerson, Dominic, Samson, and Jace formed a loose circle around the women as they knelt and sank their hands into the ground. Working in tandem, the three women murmured a spell to first close the earth and then to rejuvenate.

Mother Earth, giver of life. Darkness has descended upon you, caused you strife. Send me sage, to cleanse this air. Send me copper; send me selenium; send me iodine; spread their richness for your ground to share. Dispel this evil once and for all; in your name, heed my call.

The earth shook and settled as fresh green shoots burst through the ground. The three women sank back, exhaustion riding them hard. Emerson helped Aurelia to her feet, as Samson did the same for Lani and Dominic offered his help to Anya.

Take what you need, Emerson offered.

Give me a moment. I need to speak to Anya.

They moved closer to Emerson's brother and their young charge. "Anya, are you all right?"

"Oh, yes. I will have blood and become strong again."

"Who was that man? The one who got to you before I could?"

She looked off in the distance; for a few moments, Aurelia wondered if she would answer. "I do not know."

Jace moved closer to them. "Everyone is all right?"

"Yes." Aurelia switched her worried gaze from Anya to the healer. "We are now."

"I couldn't help but overhear. The man who saved you? I met him a couple of nights ago."

"You did? Who is he? What is his name?" Anya asked, latching onto Jace.

"Gerhard," Jace answered, eyes narrowing. "He's staying at Black Bear Lake."

Anya turned to Aurelia, eyes bright. "I must go."

Before any of them could argue, Anya was gone.

Chapter 17

Anya walked to Jade's home with disappointment stamped all over her face. She had gone to Black Bear Lake but had found no trace of the man she now knew was called Gerhard. The man she now knew, without a doubt, was her mate.

Why did he hide from her? Aurelia's mate did not do this. Neither did Reese's, or Edith's.

Did he know of her past and shun her? Would she never be good enough?

Her throat clogged with tears, Anya sank to the ground and let the rich earth soothe her. She was broken and unwanted by her mate. How could this have happened?

"Anya?" asked a voice that seemed familiar.

Looking up, Anya recognized Jared. A friend of Jace. "Oh, hello."

"What's wrong?" She must have been closer to Jade's property than she realized. She looked away, too ashamed to face a man like Jared. He crouched beside her, unable to handle a crying woman. "Did someone hurt you?"

"He hurt my heart."

"Oh, sweetheart," Jared said, pulling her into a hug. "Tell me who he is, and I'll kick his ass."

She laughed through her tears. "You would do that?"

"Of course. And I know I'd have a lot of backup."

Another stranger made his way to them, his mesmerizing aqua eyes taking in the scene he'd already witnessed in his mind. "It is not you, little one."

Anya looked up, unnerved and yet soothed by the strange man's presence. "Who are you?"

The man sat on the ground, facing Jared and Anya. "My name is Damien. I know why you cry, and I wanted to tell you that it is not your fault."

"What do you mean?"

"I'm a foreseer, little one. Do you know what that means?"

"You see the future."

"I see possible outcomes. The best course for others to be on. I have come here to tell you that you are on the right course. Your mate will come to you in time; you only need patience."

"But what have I done wrong?"

"Nothing. Absolutely nothing. Gerhard battles with his past. He does not feel worthy of you."

"This is silly. I tell him so right now."

Damien smiled. "I have no doubt you will convince him of his stupidity, but not tonight."

Sighing, Anya looked up at Jared. "You believe him?"

"That your mate is stupid for making you feel this way? Yes, I do."

Anya smiled, feeling better. "Thank you both. I will be fine now."

"I'm glad to hear it. Jared, I would also like to speak with you."

"How did you know my name?" Damien raised an eyebrow; Jared rolled his eyes. "Right. What is it?"

"Did you have plans to join the group going to Ireland?"

"I thought about it, but I think they have plenty of volunteers."

"You should go."

Jared cocked his head to the side. "Why?"

"I cannot say, only that it is the right path for you."

"Go, Jared. I believe him, so must you."

"All right. As long as you promise me there will be no more tears from you. No man is worth them."

"Okay. We have a deal." Anya stood and brushed the bramble from her clothes. Slipping her hand through the crook of first Jared's elbow and then Damien's, Anya smiled at her new friends. "I feel like Dorothy in the Oz. We should skip."

"No skipping, but I will keep an eye out for lions and tigers and bears," Jared promised.

"Oh, my," she said, laughing.

∞ ∞ ∞

AN HOUR AFTER THE BATTLE, Elementals, Gifted, and daemons gathered in Jade's backyard. Reya found Jade and checked on her first. "How are you feeling?"

"I'm fine, I promise."

"You shouldn't have been involved in that battle. And I never should have let you attempt a healing yesterday."

"Reya, I'm fine."

"It's not just you that you have to worry about."

Jade smiled. "I promise not to take any unnecessary risks."

"Deal. And I promise we will find a way to help Edith."

"I never had any doubt. So, how should we start this thing?"

"It's your yard."

With a shrug, Jade stepped back and spoke loud enough for all to hear. "Welcome, everyone. I'm so happy that we all came through the battle unscathed. I'm going to turn this over to Kayne, so he can discuss the plan for Murias."

The daemon cleared his throat. "We would like to put together a group that is willing to accompany Wynne, Emrys, Irvyn, and myself to Ireland and find the entrance to the otherworld."

"You know we're with you," Lani said, squeezing Samson's hand.

"Where Wynne goes, I go," Lenna said.

Elan crossed his arms. "And where Lenna goes, I go."

"I also volunteer," Jared said, casting a glance at one of the former shadowmen.

For a moment Reya felt concerned Jade would volunteer for this dangerous mission, but Kate cast her cousin a sideways glance and stepped forward. "Hugh and I will volunteer."

"Kate, it's going to be dangerous."

The redhead shrugged. "So is ignoring this threat. I'll leave the fighting up to those more capable, but you're going to need someone who can heal shadowmen."

Hugh took his mate's hand and nodded. "My brother and mate will have a difficult time leaving me behind."

Jade wanted to argue. They all could see it. She glanced over at Reya, and she gave Jade a minute shake of her head; Jade agreed with only the smallest grumble.

"I would also like to volunteer," Frances said, much to Jade and Lani's surprise.

Lani recovered first. "We would welcome your assistance."

"My brothers and I would also like to go," Lucius said, speaking for himself, Silas, and Augustus. He looked at Kate. "We owe you a life."

"Ireland is also my home. It has been many years, but I speak the old language and know the land better than anyone," Silas added.

"Looks like we have our team. If everyone is in agreement, there is something more I'd like to discuss," Jade said.

"What is it, love?"

"I think we should elect a leader. For too long we have been separated, Elemental traditions forgotten. We should have someone to lead us in this new phase."

"I agree, and I would like to nominate Tristan," Jared said.

Tristan looked stunned. Hugh spoke up next. "You have been our leader since we were children. I second."

Talon straightened and threw in his opinion. "You and Reya seem like the natural choice for leading. I agree."

Emerson looked at Aurelia for a moment before casting his vote. "We agree."

More and more voices spoke up. Tristan squeezed Reya's hand and spoke into her mind, unable to hide the honor he felt in his words. *This is a big responsibility for the both of us.*

You have my support. And for what it's worth, I agree with them. You are the right choice.

They shared a deep, lingering look before he inclined his head. "Thank you all for your belief and support. I humbly accept."

A brief cheer rose up; Reya shared a beaming smile with Lani. Her eyes shined with pride for her brother. "I'm so proud of you."

"Thank you, Lani," Tristan said, giving her hand a squeeze. Then, louder, he continued, "I would like to meet separately with the group infiltrating Murias. For now, are there other issues anyone would like to raise for the group?"

"We should figure out a way to reach out to more Elementals, those in hiding or on their own," Jade said.

"Gatherings like this are a wonderful idea. I have found family here that I didn't know existed. Though my sister is lost to me, there may be others in my line, as evidenced by Jade's brother-in-law. There is hope for us all, yet." Grey spoke up for the first time, and there were several nods of agreement. Grey and Micah had discovered their connection at the rehearsal dinner, and Reya had a feeling the former shadowman would be staying in the area.

"We need to continue to search for Elementals, not only to find our missing family but to give us all hope," Tristan said. "Hope is what will brighten even the darkest soul, keep them from turning. I have found my sister after more than a century of believing she was lost to me. If we work together, we can restore what once was.

"However, we face a much larger problem—there are still shadowmen who need to be found and saved, and the daemons who seem to be behind much of the darkness in the world. After we liberate any sympathizers from Murias, we must prepare for war. We need to have a plan in place and a way to communicate. When this threat rises—as I believe it will, especially now that we have taken back our brothers from their grasp and once we succeed in Mag Mell—we need to band together to stop them."

"Any shadowmen that are found are welcome in California," Kate said, "if any of you come across one and are able to transport him. If you need me to come to you, I will do so."

"Thank you, Kate. Are there any among us with an ability that would assist in finding shadowmen?" Tristan asked. A few raised their hands but didn't want to speak in front of the group. Tristan nodded. "We will speak privately. Thank you all for your belief in me. I will do my best by you."

Another cheer rose as Reya took in the determined faces surrounding her. Too long these men—and women—had lived alone, shrouded in darkness. Too long they lived in fear. It was time for a new beginning, for a better future for their children.

"I'm open to any and all ideas," Tristan added, spreading his arms wide. "If you wish not to speak in front of us all, please find myself or Reya at any time."

At that point several groups began talking amongst themselves. A former shadowmen Reya hadn't met yet made his way over, bowing courteously before shaking Tristan's hand.

"My name is Damien Nikora," he introduced himself. "I didn't want to speak about this in front of the group, but I may be able to assist with the daemons."

"How so?" Tristan asked, moving closer to his mate and wrapping an arm around her waist.

Damien's strange aqua eyes switched to Reya. "I am also a foreseer."

"Really?" she said on a breath, instantly excited. The power was new to her, and she felt like she would never fully grasp all of the complexities of seeing the future. Having someone to speak with, possibly learn from, would be incredible.

"Yes," he said, dipping his head in acknowledgment. "As was my father."

His statement floored Reya and Tristan, as male foreseers were exceptionally rare—but a second-generation male foreseer? Tristan and Reya exchanged a glance. *Have you come across this before?*

The legends are so scarce as it is, Tristan replied. Without missing a beat, Tristan continued aloud, "We would love to hear more. Reya is newly into her powers and unfortunately never knew her parents."

"You've been training on your own?" Damien asked, shock in his eyes.

"Yes," Reya answered, suddenly feeling self-conscious. "I didn't have much choice."

"No, I suppose not. I would be happy to work with you. I've been thinking of setting out on my own, anyway, to look for my sister."

"Your sister?" Reya asked, eyes wide. Part of the legend of male foreseers was that they were only able to conceive once, and instead of twins like Elementals tended to be, a single child.

"Yes. She is younger than I am, and it's been many centuries since I have seen her. She carries the same gene."

Sibling foreseers? Reya sent to Tristan.

"You must hail from a very powerful family, indeed," Tristan said with the utmost respect.

From her own experience, that may not even be the half of it. Reya was able to foresee events, like her father, travel with her spirit, like her mother, and she also had her own power—healing. *I wonder what else he can do.* It seemed rude to ask, though her curiosity brimmed.

"We are heading back to New Zealand after the wedding. We would love to have you join us."

"It has been many years since I have been to the place of my birth. I will make what arrangements I must and accompany you," Damien said, bowing deeply again before disappearing back into the crowd.

He's from New Zealand. Have you heard of his family?

It is not familiar. More and more I am grateful for what Jade and Kate have done, Tristan said. *I am so honored that everyone has put their faith in us.*

In you, Reya corrected with a twinkle in her eye.

I am nothing without you by my side.

Though their thoughts were private their gazes were locked, and Reya felt herself sinking into his dark eyes. Luckily, before it could get out of control, someone cleared their throat.

"Not to interrupt, but..."

"What is it, Jared?" Reya asked politely. He had a real knack for disrupting private moments.

"The Murias group is ready to meet with you now."

Tristan nodded his thanks, straightened his back, and prepared for his first meeting as a leader.

Chapter 18

It wasn't fair.

While their parents went to some big meeting, Kai got stuck with the babies. She was twelve years old. Practically an adult! Everything inside her said she should be out there, helping to plan. It's not like she didn't know what was going on. They were putting a group together to infiltrate Murias and free any captives. How cool was that?

Kai's parents had been acting strange ever since the daemon attack on their home. They knew she had great power inside her—her dad said as much. But they both worried for her and wanted her to enjoy her childhood.

Too young to fight, too old to color with her sisters. Speaking of sisters...

Kai looked at Kateri as she had often since the night of the final battle. She had an old soul. Kai had always been able to see that, even when she was being nosy and annoying. What Kai hadn't bet on was one of the baddest beings to ever exist living inside her.

All that knowledge, all that power. She couldn't pull it out at will—they were both sure it only manifested when it did because they would have been sunk otherwise.

Biroġ of the Mountain. You can bet Kai and her adopted siblings all read every piece of material on her that they could find.

"Are you mad at your sister?"

The voice startled Kai. She looked at Kalinda and tried to soften her glare. "No. I was just thinking."

"About how we're stuck here instead of with the others?"

Now this was a girl who understood. Kalinda Scott, daughter of Malakai and sister to Daku. Daku, only two years older than Kai and Kalinda, and *he* got to go with the adults. "Exactly."

Kalinda settled on the stair. They watched the other kids playing in the basement, envious of their ignorant bliss. "Pearl's really nice and all, but this sucks."

"Tell me about it. Why does your brother get to go?"

"He's considered an adult by our people. He went through his koradji training."

"Are you going to do that, too?"

She shrugged. "Probably."

Kai studied her curiously. Something in her voice made Kai think she knew exactly what her future would hold. "What is it?"

"No one else knows," Kalinda said with a sigh. "But I—I already have the visions."

"You do?" Kai's eyes widened and she grinned. "Tell me about them!"

"They're not some great gift," Kalinda said in a whisper. "We're not supposed to get them until our training!"

"That just means you're really powerful and that's awesome."

"I guess so."

"We should practice."

"Are you crazy? No."

Excitement bubbled up. Finally, something to *do*. "Come on, it'll be fun. We'll cast a protection circle—I know how to do that."

"We're not supposed to."

"Come on, please?" When that didn't work, Kai gripped Kalinda's wrist, made her look into her doe eyes. "Kalinda, I have a great power in me, too. I know it, my family knows it. I have a destiny. I just want an idea what it is."

She shook her head, but Kai could tell she had Kalinda on the line. "What if you don't like what I see?"

"I won't blame you, if that's what you're worried about. It's not like you're the one making it happen. You're just the messenger."

Her lips twitched. "All right. Let's do it."

Together they ran up the stairs, pausing just before pushing open the door. "Distract Pearl while I get what we need from the kitchen."

"Okay," Kalinda agreed with wide, excited eyes.

They went their separate ways. Kai found sea salt on the stove, a candle and some incense in a drawer, and used a copper mug from the cabinet to collect water from the tap. Treasures in hand, Kai signaled Kalinda to meet her outside. Kai could hear her tell Pearl that they were going to swing—Pearl had a huge collection of playground equipment for her kids—before Kalinda followed her out the door.

Kai led her to a piece of the yard that would be covered from curious eyes should anyone happen to glance out the window. The sun had just begun to set; the moon had already risen. Perfect.

Handing Kalinda the water and incense stick, Kai crouched to the south and lit the candle. "I ask the element of fire to bless this circle." Gesturing Kalinda to stand in the west with the cup of water, Kai said, "I ask the element of water to bless this circle." Sprinkling the salt to the north, she repeated the entreaty to earth before standing across from Kalinda and grasping the incense in her own hands and asking for the wind's blessing.

A subtle ripple of energy surrounded them; Kai could almost see the soothing waves in the air. Kalinda gasped with the beauty of it. "I didn't really think this would work."

"It's your turn," Kai said. "Can I do anything to help?"

"I'll let you know." Closing her eyes, Kalinda took deep breaths to steady herself. When she opened them again, it didn't seem as if anything had changed. She peered into the water and let out a frustrated grunt. "It's not working."

Somewhere behind Kai a door opened and closed. A surge of power exploded from their chests. Startled, she looked around to see Kateri holding Nicola, who stared at the girls from a few feet away. He was just a baby, but right then he had an intelligence in his eyes well beyond his years.

Kai had overheard what he could do. Just being near meant he could boost their power.

"What are you doing?" Kateri asked.

"Never mind. Just go back inside."

"Whoa," Kalinda murmured, staring down at the bowl of water glowing in her palms. "It's working. This feels...weird."

Kai forgot all about her sister and focused back on her new friend. "What do you see?" She reached out with one hand. The moment their skin touched the world around them changed.

Gone was the large backyard filled with toys. Gone was the fading light of day. They opened their eyes to another world.

Underground, judging by the dim light and smell of earth and stone. Kalinda and Kai looked around in wonder.

What is this place? Kalinda asked, neither out loud nor in Kai's mind. It seemed they were connected on a level neither had ever experienced before or could explain.

I have no idea.

By mutual agreement they went deeper into what they discovered to be a cave system. The room they were in opened to a larger one; here they found sconces filled with fire to illuminate the cavernous space.

Three women stood in a circle, chanting with their eyes closed. Kai and Kalinda snuck closer and gasped with surprise. *It's us. We're adults.*

They weren't alone. The third woman that stood with them had pale skin—a stark contrast to her bright red hair. It fell like flames down her back. Power sparked in her eyes as she intoned a spell. Adult-them linked hands, murmured along with her.

The ground shook as if an earthquake had been unleashed. Stones and stalactites tumbled and crashed to the ground, but the three women stood strong, seemingly unaffected by nature's force. Two huge sarcophagi emerged from the earth and came to rest on either side of the group of three. The ground settled and the women opened their eyes.

Kalinda and Kai snapped back to reality and fell on their butts. When Kai looked over at Nicola, he sat on the ground happily digging through the dirt, unaffected by the shared vision.

"What *was* that?" Kalinda asked.

Kai had more questions. Who was that woman, who were the mummies, and why the *hell* were they resurrecting them?

∞ ∞ ∞

DAKU LAY AWAKE IN HIS room at the inn. He'd been sharing the space with his sister, but she was at a sleepover at Pearl's, and he appreciated the privacy. During the brief but fierce battle and the meeting that followed, Daku had put on a brave face, but now that he was alone, he could admit that he'd been scared and might still be in shock.

He knew that he had never really been in danger; between his parents and the Elementals he'd come to know, he'd been well protected. Still, talking about a battle and seeing one first hand were vastly different experiences.

For the last hour since he'd come back to his room, he'd been laying awake, staring at the ceiling, and reliving every terrifying second. Strangely, he didn't feel the need to avoid violence in the future. Instead, he felt an overwhelming need to be prepared.

After spending his whole life prepping for and completing his koradji training, Daku knew it was time to start honing his physical abilities. He carried both the magic of his people and the Gifted gene; it was a strong possibility he would convert to become an Elemental at some point in his life. Not just a possibility—Daku knew it like he knew the sun would rise in the morning.

When he traveled with his spirit, Daku existed in the past, present, and future simultaneously. Not everything was set in stone, but one thing was absolutely certain for Daku; he would not remain a human forever.

His thoughts flickered toward his mystery woman, as they did so often during his day. He had been drawn to her spirit for as long as he could remember, but he had no clue who she was. She never responded in any way, never acknowledged his presence with so much of a flicker of awareness in her eyes. Still, he found himself seeking her out, day after day, night after night. He didn't know who she was, but she was as vitally important to him as his own family.

Daku knew he needed to tell someone about her. Someone who could help her. She was in danger, and Daku had no idea where she was or how to find her. He should tell one of the Elementals—Tristan, perhaps. He would make sure the mystery woman was found and safe.

The idea of sharing her frightened Daku more than the image of battling daemons. Still, he knew it was time. If anyone could help him, help her, they would be in the group gathered for Jade's wedding.

He closed his eyes and used his breathing techniques to let the world around him slip away. Without needing direction, his soul found hers. Her condition seemed much the same, and he tried once more to reach out, to get her to speak. If she would just tell him where she was, who she was, he could find her on his own.

It was another fruitless attempt, and Daku came back into his own body, knowing he'd run out of excuses.

He would ask for help before returning home.

Chapter 19

The night had finally arrived. Jade and Talon would soon be married, tied together in human eyes as well as Elemental. Lani walked through the park that would hold the event, a canopy of lights and rows of chairs already placed, a pile of wood awaiting a spark of fire to be lit.

While a few from the catering company did last-minute checks, Jade's family and other guests were away, getting ready for the night—except for one lone figure crouched at the edge of the chairs.

"Frances, what are you doing?" Lani asked, eyes narrowed.

He had the foresight to look sheepish but gave her his best little boy grin. "It's a surprise for Jade." Crossing her arms, Lani waited none so patiently for him to explain. With a sigh, he did. "With all the non-Elemental guests, she wouldn't be able to have a full ceremony. So, I thought I would concoct a spell covering the entire area—any who enter here will take whatever they see in stride."

"You mean, humans who witness magic won't freak out?" Lani asked.

"Basically, yes."

She was frozen in shock. "Wow, Frances, that's…"

"Awesome?" he suggested.

"Yes. And thoughtful. Jade will love it."

"I got the idea when I figured out a way to cover the daemon's horns. Same principle, really. I spoke with Malakai before trying this so he could plan out the ceremony. It should be all set."

On impulse, Lani reached out and pulled Frances into a hug. He seemed less surprised by it than she was. "I'm proud of you. You're maturing into a man any woman would be proud to call a mate."

"Thanks, Lani," he replied, his voice thick.

Not wanting to embarrass him, Lani stepped back with a wink. "Let's go find Jade, and you can tell her about your gift."

He nodded and manfully fought back the tears that were threatening to spill. Lani led the way, taking a shortcut from the park to Jade's home, where she would be in the stages of getting dressed. Samson was with Talon, doing whatever it was groomsmen did, but she could constantly feel their connection, which was reassuring.

Everything okay? Samson asked, sensing her thoughts.

Now it is, Lani sent back. *How are things on your end?*

Talon is dressed and ready to go.

Jade should be shortly, she replied as she arrived at the bride's door. After a cursory knock, Lani poked her head in.

Jade and Pearl were the only ones in the room, surprisingly. That would probably only last a few minutes, so Lani took advantage. "Jade, Frances would like to speak to you. Pearl, would you mind giving them a minute?"

"Sure." The younger woman smiled, setting aside the curling iron she'd been using on Jade. "Just a minute though, we're almost finished."

She joined Lani in the hall as Frances nodded his thanks and went inside. Though she could listen if she wanted to, Lani decided to give them privacy.

Frances had a special connection to Jade, since she was the one who saved him from being a shadowman. Lani had always thought Jade felt particularly protective of Frances, as well, since he was the first shadowman she'd saved.

Even though he still drove her nuts, Lani had come to think of Frances like a little brother. And now that she'd found her real brother, Lani was excited to visit her home for the first time in centuries—and to share that with Samson.

It was still amazing to her how much her life had changed over the course of a couple years. From the moment she met Jade, suddenly Lani was no longer alone in the world.

"Oh, she looks so beautiful!" Pearl said as she closed the door, dabbing delicately under her eyes. "I just know I'm going to be a blubbering mess."

"I'm sure you won't be the only one," Lani said in consolation. "You wore the waterproof mascara, right?"

"Always," Pearl said with a laugh.

It was only a minute later that Frances left the room, his eyes red-rimmed. Without making eye contact, he thanked them and hurried down the hall. No, Pearl would not be the only one to shed some tears today.

Pearl and Lani went to Jade's side and were soon joined by her mom and her two older sisters. Everyone else was getting seated, the ceremony set to begin just as the sun dipped below the horizon.

"Honey, you look so beautiful," Madeline said, resting a hand over her heart as Pearl curled the last chunk of hair.

"Thanks, Mom," Jade said, turning to face us as a group. "Thank you all. Without you, none of this would be happening."

"You mean the wedding itself or you and Talon?" Pearl winked, making them all laugh.

"Talon and I would have found each other even without your meddling," Jade shot back. "Mostly, I meant the wedding. Everything is gorgeous and so perfect. Thank you." She reached her arms out and they all gathered together in a group hug, careful not to muss their outfits or hair. When they stepped back, Jade gave a determined nod. "All right, let's do this."

The group of women made their way outside, where a stretch limo waited in the driveway. They piled in, careful with Jade's dress, and pulled up to the back of the rows of guests at the park. Madeline met Talon outside and Jade's dad helped her from the vehicle. Madeline wore a pretty, light pink lace dress and tossed them a smile as she looped her arm through Talon's, starting off the procession.

Pearl, with Micah, was the next to make the walk. The bridesmaid dresses were knee-length and turquoise, with the same strip of white leather and beads across the stomach as Jade's dress. Once Pearl reached the halfway point down the aisle, Emma stepped out with Rick, then Amber with Jack followed suit.

Finally, it was Lani's turn. Samson waited for her with a huge grin, warming her from the inside out.

"Hi there, beautiful," he whispered as her hand fit through his arm.

"Hello yourself, handsome."

The aisle had been strewn with flower petals, the rows of guests spanning out as far as a human eye could see. A small fire pit had been lit in the front of the aisle, where Samson and Lani split to walk to their side.

Malakai Scott, along with Viktor Blackfoot, waited at the front as coefficients. Talon—wearing a black tux with a white and turquoise blanket that had been handmade by Neveah and Emilia wrapped around his waist and draped over one shoulder—shook Samson's hand as he took his place beside the groom.

Once Lani took her place beside Jade's sisters, everyone turned to face the end of the aisle, the crowd standing as the music changed. Jade began her march, squeezing her dad's arm tight. Though the space had been filled with her family and closest friends, she only had eyes for Talon. Jade's dad transferred her hand from his arm to Talon's, shaking Talon's hand and murmuring something in his ear that was too low for anyone but Elementals to hear.

"I couldn't imagine a better man for my little girl to spend her life with," Isaac said to Talon. Then, with a kiss on Jade's cheek, he found his seat beside his wife.

"We come together today to bless the union of Talon Wolfchild and Jade Callaghan," Malakai began. Lani knew Malakai and Viktor had worked together to blend the two cultures, along with Frances' help for the magical aspects.

"First, a blessing from the Apache people," Viktor said loudly, placing a hand over Jade and Talon's joined ones. "Now you will feel no rain, for each of you will be shelter for the other. Now you will feel no cold, for each of you will be warmth to the other. Now there will be no loneliness, for each of you will be companion to the other. Now you are two persons, but there is only one life before you. May beauty surround you both in the journey ahead and through all the years. May happiness be your companion and your days together be good and long upon the earth."

"We ask for Talon and Jade the blessings of Nature's Elements," Malakai continued as Viktor stepped back. "Air, Fire, Water, and Earth. We do this that they may fully come to understand the lessons that each element has to offer."

"Spirit of Fire, we ask that Talon and Jade's passion for each other, and for life, remain ever strong and vital. May they take on each new day with boldness and courage. As Fire clears the way for new growth, may they know that this power is theirs; to create change and bring richness and a true love of life," Viktor said, his words bringing life to the bonfire. It swelled and crackled, causing several people in the aisle to cringe back in surprise before Malakai continued.

"Spirit of Air, keep open the lines of communication between this couple. May their future be as bright as the dawn on the horizon. As Air flows freely between and through us all, may their hearts and minds and souls come to know the world and each other in this manner. Seeing not only with their eyes, may they together grow wise with wisdom." A gentle breeze swept through the crowd, connecting each and every soul, wrapping them all in a warm cocoon.

"We ask the spirits of water, that their love for each other, like the serenity of the deep blue ocean, be the oasis that forever surrounds our bride and groom. May they be well-loved, and love well, letting the surety with which Water flows on its journey to the sea, flowing over rocks or around trees, even turning to vapor and riding a cloud, ever serve as a reminder that with love all is well and will endure." Here Viktor presented the wedding chalice to Talon, waiting for them both to take a sip before Malakai continued.

"Spirit of Earth, we ask that you give unto those you see standing before you this day, the rock-solid place to stand and fulfill their destiny. May their journey mirror the vast planes and fertile fields, expansive and alive. May they find the right seeds to sow in order to ensure a bountiful harvest." Flowers sprang from the earth, covering the ground in their beautiful blooms. From the crowd, little Leia cooed with delight.

"Father, Mother, Divine Spirit: we ask your continued blessings upon this couple, upon their union and upon their family and friends who have gathered here to celebrate this joyous event with them. May they become one in truth and forever revel in the magic that is love," Viktor said.

Malakai stepped forward, pulling leather cords from his pocket that had been prepared by Viktor and Santiago. Wrapping them first around Talon's wrist, he did the same with Jade. "Remember as your hands are fasted, these are not the ties that bind. The role already taken by the song in your hearts shall now be strengthened by the vows you take. All things of the material world eventually return to the Earth, unlike the bond and the connection your spirits share, which is destined to ascend to the heavens. May you be forever as one in the passion and fire of you."

"Talon," Viktor said proudly. "Do you swear to uphold Jade's life and happiness above your own, for all time?"

"I do," Talon answered in a steady voice.

"Jade, do you swear to uphold Talon's life and happiness above your own, for all time?"

"I do," Jade replied with a watery smile.

Viktor added another Apache blessing, as their hands were still tied. "Treat yourselves and each other with respect and remind yourselves often of what brought you together. Give the highest priority to the tenderness, gentleness, and kindness that your connection deserves. When frustration, difficulties, and fear assail your relationship, as they threaten all relationships at one time or another, remember to focus on what is right between you, not only the part which seems wrong. In this way, you can ride out the storms when clouds hide the face of the sun in your lives—remembering that even if you lose sight of it for a moment, the sun is still there. And if each of you takes responsibility for the quality of your life together, it will be marked by abundance and delight."

Talon and Jade smiled at each other, then at Viktor, nodding their agreement. Finally, Malakai spoke the words they'd all been waiting to hear. "You are now as your hearts have always known you to be: husband and wife. Talon, kiss your bride!"

Chapter 20

E dith moved through the crowd, her legs trembling with trepidation. She had come to apologize to Jade and Talon, and to Jace. Though she had acted rudely in order to keep Jade's secret, she still felt horrible about what had happened.

The park had been transformed into a scene worthy of a fairy-tale. Strings of lights gave the party a soft glow, while couples twirled around a bonfire that had been spelled for the smoke and sparks to rise straight into the air before dispersing.

She could feel the low hum of power from so many magical beings in one area, but none that felt dark. It was so positive, so invigorating.

It helped her put one foot in front of the other.

She'd worn a red dress with a daring neckline and off the shoulder sleeves; the waist hugged her curves before flaring out to the floor. To cover some of her skin, Edith had picked out elbow-length white gloves. Not only did they make her feel less risqué, but they also helped her make contact with others without accidentally seeing their entire life's memories.

Before she could make her way to Jade and Talon, Edith spotted Jace. He must have felt her presence, for his gaze found her with unerring accuracy. She stopped, just feet away from the dancing, frozen to the ground.

He walked to her as if in slow motion. Or perhaps her brain had stopped firing on all circuits, for Jace wore a black suit that had been tailored to his toned form. Edith's mouth went dry, and she licked her lips, her gaze sweeping to his feet and back again.

"Edith." Such emotion in his tone when he said her name. "You look amazing."

"You look rather handsome yourself."

"I'm so glad you decided to come."

"Yes. About that. Jace..."

He stepped closer, taking her gloved hand between his palms. "Yes?"

"I apologize for the way I acted."

"You have nothing to apologize for."

"I do. I acted horribly, after you did so much to help Anya and everyone so willing to help me and..."

"Taku tama muna. Do you not know by now? I would do anything for you."

Edith stared at him, her emotions swirling through her like a maelstrom. She didn't know if she might laugh or cry; stay or run. The next words she blurted out were a surprise to them both. "Dance with me."

For a moment Jace looked stunned, but it didn't take him long to recover. Moving her hand to the crook of his arm, he inclined his head. "It would be my pleasure."

They moved into the throng of couples dancing. Edith recognized Kate, dancing with a man that must be her father; Reya with Tristan, their twins between them; Jade and Talon, with eyes only for each other. So many more Edith didn't know.

Anya, laughing with a man who must be Hugh's twin; Aurelia and Emerson, swaying in each other's arms, even though they stayed on the peripheral of the party. Reese, eyes closed and looking absolutely blissful in her mate's embrace.

"This is so lovely," Edith said. "So much happiness. So much joy."

"We all deserve that."

"We do." Edith braced herself, looked Jace fully in the eye. "I still need more time, but I want this for us. For me."

"Take as long as you need. You are worth the wait."

Once again overcome by emotion, Edith rested her head against Jace's chest. She didn't feel worth it, but she vowed to become the person Jace already thought her to be.

$$\infty \quad \infty \quad \infty$$

MAY I HAVE THIS DANCE, my lady?"

Valentina stared in shock at Embry. She'd been sitting with Raven, minding her own business. She'd done so well to avoid Embry...until now. His unfailing manners and sexy stare had Valentina's cheeks burning bright with color. Though she heard a lewd remark and giggle from Raven, Valentina accepted Embry's hand and let him lead her to the dance floor.

"I'm not much of a dancer." She felt compelled to warn him.

"Then you've never had a proper lead," Embry answered with a devilish grin, capturing one hand while his other slid around her waist.

They began to move, and though she stumbled slightly at first, Valentina tried to relax and follow along. Once she gave up trying to think through what she was doing, Embry easily twirled her along the ground.

The heat from his hands seared into her, right through the thin material of her dress. Her heart beat fast, but not from the exertion of the dance—from the way his perfectly tailored suit fit him so snugly.

"Your heart is racing," Embry murmured. "Is it from my dancing skills, or is it me?"

"Aren't you full of yourself," Valentina said with a smirk.

He bent his head low until his lips were at her ear. A tingle spread down her spine and tickled her toes. "My heart beats quicker when I'm near you," he whispered against her neck.

Every nerve ending went on full alert. Whatever existed between them was strong—and undeniable. "I'm sorry I've been avoiding you. I just couldn't deal, you know?"

He looked at her with confusion. "Deal?"

"This thing between us is crazy. I don't know how to handle it. I have absolutely no experience in this area."

"Good." He flashed his teeth in what could be considered more of a threat than a smile.

Valentina rolled her eyes. "Helpful."

"I apologize. What can I do to help?"

Stop looking so sexy. Too late, Valentina realized she'd projected that thought into his mind. He smiled fully now, male satisfaction coming off him in waves. *Stop!*

I'm afraid I cannot control how I look to my mate. If it helps, I feel the same way for you.

No, it doesn't help!

His eyes lit with amusement, Embry leaned close. "Let's start slow. I would like to get to know you better."

"Okay. Okay. That I can deal with."

As the song came to a close, Embry dipped her low, his mouth hovering just above hers. Their eyes locked, and Valentina stared at him, her emotions warring with themselves while he held her completely under his spell.

He brought her back up slowly, though he had yet to relinquish his hold. Their gazes held as he began to close the distance between them, until his lips were just a hairsbreadth away.

My family... she breathed into his mind.

We are blurred from view.

Before she could argue, his lips were on hers. He tasted exactly how she thought he would—like pure sin and heaven wrapped up in one delectably sexy package. Valentina pressed against him, and his arms tightened around her waist until she felt each firm muscle imprinted against her softer form.

The world blurred and spun out, no longer existing in this new reality that Embry created with his mouth alone. She felt breathless, but for the air he breathed into her. Her limbs were weak and useless, turning to putty in his capable hands.

Valentina pulled away, dazed and momentarily confused. Their surroundings slowly came back into focus, but she still couldn't tear her gaze from his handsome face.

He stared right back, wonder lighting his eyes from deep gray to nearly silver. His hand reached up and he brushed his thumb along her swollen lower lip. *I have found heaven; it is right here in my arms.*

Valentina's heart skittered and then began to pound, his words running through her veins like liquid fire. She forgot how to breathe, how to speak, how to think.

"I realize you still have much to decide, and I expect nothing of you. Thank you for this dance. I will treasure the memory of it forever." Embry released his hold, bringing her knuckles to his mouth for a kiss. He turned and began to walk away, leaving her feeling bereft.

So much for taking it slow.

∞ ∞ ∞

EVERYTHING HAD TURNED OUT SO perfect. The bonfire still burned brightly while couples danced in the now-open space. A ring of torches provided warmth and light and the most romantic ambiance Jade could have asked for.

Talon spun her in a dizzying twirl before pulling his new wife tight against him. They'd had their first dance—they'd asked the band to play the same song that they'd danced to back on their first date. Talon had surprised Jade with a trip to Madison in his very fast car, and they'd eaten together on a patio as the sun set. Even though she'd thought he was crazy at the time for asking, Jade had danced with him among the tables as a band played.

Since the first song, Jade had danced with her dad, many relatives, and even more Elementals. Talon had taken his turn with her mom and sisters, along with the ladies in his family. Finally, Jade got Talon all to herself.

Do you think we would be missed if we snuck away for a few minutes?

Jade smiled up at him. *Too bad if we are.*

Grinning, the co-conspirators blurred their images and snuck off into the woods. Once they reached the tree line, Talon scooped Jade into his arms and took off at a nauseating run. She buried her nose against his neck, loving the way he held her so tightly.

When Talon stopped, Jade looked up and stared around for a moment before recognition sank in. "Talon..."

"You know where we are?"

"Of course. This is where I first saw you in all your shirtless glory."

"It is where you fainted for the first time, being stunned by my attractiveness."

Jade slapped his arm playfully. "You know perfectly well I don't faint. Oh, this was such a nice surprise."

Tears welled in her eyes. Stupid hormones. Talon set her on her feet so he could wrap her in a hug. "Oh, love, please don't cry. Even happy tears. I cannot take them."

"I've been so excited and nervous for this day. Excited to commit to you in front of all our family and friends, nervous about being the center of attention."

"I know you haven't been feeling well. Weddings can be very stressful."

"It wasn't the wedding. At least, not just the wedding."

"Jade?" Talon's eyebrows twitched in confusion, and she smiled, knowing she'd finally managed to surprise him.

"Talon, we're pregnant."

For a beat, complete silence reigned. When her words sunk in, Talon's eyes grew wide as saucers before he tightened his hold, lifted Jade from her feet, and twirled her in a circle. The world blurred as she let out a lilting laugh.

Talon set Jade down and his mouth claimed hers. Such delight radiated from Talon that Jade could hardly breathe. When he finally pulled away, his smile rivaled the stars above. "Really? We're going to have a baby?"

Jade nodded, tears already falling. "Babies, Talon. We're having twins...twin boys."

And then they were spinning again. Their exuberant laughs rose and twined together, filling the night with infinite happiness. When she finally regained her composure, Jade held out her hand. Her husband clasped it tightly. "Come on, let's go tell everyone else."

"Before we do, there's one thing I have to say."

Jade waited, her absolute joy shining through her eyes like two bright beacons of hope. "What's that?"

"I love you, Jade Wolfchild."

After Dusk

Book Seven and a Half of the Gifted Series

Ana Ban

Chapter 1

Sure, it was early. But I hadn't slept all night—not one freaking minute. The reception had gone well into the night, but even after the most die-hard had called it, I paced my room in indecision.

The kiss Embry and I had shared after our one dance had been explosive, world-rocking—life-altering. It had awoken things in me I didn't even know existed.

It had kept me up all night.

And now, I had to tell my family the decision I'd come to barely an hour before.

Whipping eggs in a bowl, I eyed the bacon already sizzling in a pan. Food always seemed to be a good buffer with my family, so I made a lot of it. Fresh fruit cut up in a bowl, bread ready to be dipped in the egg batter, and frozen hash browns heating in a pan.

Josiah—my brother and, oddly enough, one of my closest friends—slept upstairs with his wife, Tayen. Raven, my best friend since before we could walk, occupied the third bedroom.

The rest of the clan stayed in other houses on the same property. Atienn and Chayton, along with their sisters Nova and Tala, were right next door. We were the closest in age, and though we weren't first cousins, we still treated each other as such. Domingo and Emilia, their parents, had their own small cottage next to that. Viktor and Niko, with their kids Kai, Kateri, Koko, and Kaiah, had taken over the largest home on the property.

Samson and Lani had a little cabin, plus Neveah and Santiago took up another. Lenna and Elan—and, if my eyes hadn't deceived me, Wynne—slept in a two-bedroom cabin beside that.

And I had to tell them all about my decision.

A bleary-eyed Raven clomped down the stairs, too tired to glare, but I understood her annoyance was implied. Slipping onto a stool at the kitchen island, she grumbled, "What are you doing?"

"Making breakfast!" I told her brightly.

She winced as if this hurt her head. "Why?"

"Because I couldn't sleep, so I thought I'd do something nice for everyone." Raven studied me with a critical eye. She knew me better than anyone else in the world, and I turned away from her unusually sharp gaze to flip the bacon.

"At six o'clock in the morning," she said with no small amount of censure. "After a night of drinking and dancing. What's going on?"

"Nothing," I lied lightly.

"Puh-lease." Dragging the word into two syllables, she rolled her eyes and clasped her hands on the counter. "Even without my gift, after all these years, you think you can lie to me?"

Hunching my shoulders, I turned to face her. Her wide, chocolate eyes watched me carefully. "I want to talk to everyone at once. Would you help me gather them all together? We can eat outside."

There were several picnic tables near the small lake, and it was the only space large enough for us all to sit together. Raven nodded mutely, sliding off the stool again to get dressed and wake the rest of the family.

That had always been one of my favorite things about Raven—though she liked to be nosy and could be a little bossy, when it was important, she could keep her mouth shut. She also always came through for me.

I finished cooking while an annoyed Josiah made his way down the stairs with Tayen right behind him. Raven bounded down next, heading out to start the wake-up calls.

"Valentina, this is our vacation. We're supposed to be able to sleep in," Josiah said.

"I know, I know. You can go back to sleep after we eat. Here, take this outside."

Shoving the pan of French toast into his hands, I handed off the plate of bacon to Tayen. She merely smiled at me, amusement lighting her eyes.

Tayen had an uncanny ability to read people, an ability that would manifest tenfold if she were ever converted to become an Elemental. Lani and Samson had explained that world to us—though we'd already had an idea, with the stories passed down in our tribe. Most of us didn't believe, but I always had.

After all, I had descended from the original Elementals of the Apache Tribe. Magic flowed through my veins.

I grabbed more platters of food and made my way outside, where my brother and Tayen were spreading plates and utensils out for everyone. Atienn, Chayton, Nova, and Tala were outside, still wearing pajamas. Neveah and Santiago were next—I had a feeling they were already up—as were Samson and Lani, who looked the freshest out of the lot.

Must be nice to not get hangovers.

Elan came out of his cabin, Lenna and Wynne in tow. Viktor, Niko, and their family were last to arrive, as they had the most to wrangle. Everyone looked exhausted but curious, and I grabbed Raven to help me carry out the last of the meal, plus carafes of coffee.

"Thanks for breakfast," Santiago said first, "but what's this all about?"

Everyone scooped food onto their plates in various states of wakefulness. Though I shook with nerves, I took a deep breath and stood before them all.

"I'm sorry to wake you all so early," I began, pausing when my statement met with several grumbles. "But I have an announcement to make."

"You're not pregnant, are you?" my brother asked, looking slightly terrified.

"What? No!" I exclaimed, appalled. Just who did he think I would have gotten pregnant with? "I—I've made a decision."

"Out with it, Val," Nova shouted. "Some of us need our beauty sleep."

"Speak for yourself," Chayton replied. "I'm always pretty."

This earned him a slap on his shoulder, and I rolled my eyes. I loved my family, I loved my family, I loved my family…

"I'm staying in Sun Valley!" I blurted out.

Shocked silence met my announcement. Something akin to indigestion clogged my throat as I took in all of their stares. Josiah found his voice first. "What? Why?"

"I'll tell you why," Raven said with a smirk. "Because of a man."

On his feet now, Josiah slammed his palms against the table. "What man?"

Sighing, I sent my best friend a glare, which she subsequently ignored. "I've—I've met my mate."

The air thickened, electricity and power crackling and raising all the little hairs on my arms and neck. Embry appeared beside me, his arms crossed and a glare on his face. "Who dares to cause my mate distress?"

Silence reigned over the large gathering, most pausing mid-chew to stare at the newcomer. Josiah marched right up to Embry, chest puffed out and a red haze closing over his eyes. "You don't get to speak to me like that, and you sure as hell don't get to take my sister away."

"My mate has made a decision to be near me," Embry replied, not backing down.

I'd had about all the male posturing I could handle. Stepping between them, I placed a hand against each of their chests and shoved. "Back the hell up! What is wrong with you?"

I will not allow anyone to speak to you that way, Embry whispered into my mind while my brother spoke aloud simultaneously. "He has no right to come here and—"

Cutting Josiah off, I held up a finger and said sternly, "This is my life and my decision. I've chosen to stay in Sun Valley because I've been wanting to leave the reservation for some time, anyway. And yes, my decision has partly to do with Embry—I would like to get to know him better." Spinning around to face the man who made my heart race, I continued in my rant. "And you. Just because you think we're mates gives you no right to dictate to me or my family. If we get to know each other, and I find I actually like you, then we can talk about having a relationship. Until then, notch down the machismo."

I could practically see both men's egos deflate. Embry offered a stiff nod. "I apologize. This is new for me, as well. Please forgive my intrusion."

"You've got your work cut out for you with this one," Josiah replied, the hint of a smile on his face. "I don't envy you that."

Rolling my eyes, I pointed at the copious amounts of food lined up on the picnic table. The rest of the family watched the encounter with expressions ranging from fascination to fear. "The food's getting cold. Embry, you're welcome to join us. Everyone else, start eating.".

Raven stood as I plopped onto the bench, sagging as all my nervous energy dissipated. She cleared her throat delicately before speaking. "I'm going to stay with Valentina." There were more protests, but I found myself speechless. My best friend had managed to shock me. Raven held out a placating hand, giving her parents an apologetic look. "With Samson and Lani leaving first for Ireland and then New Zealand, I feel it is time for me to try something new, as well. It's not forever," she promised, still looking directly at her parents, "but I feel it's the right thing for me."

Santiago and Neveah exchanged a look that spoke volumes without a sound. Her mother finally said, "Though we would prefer to keep you with us forever, we understand."

Raven ran over to them and practically tackled them with a hug while Viktor cleared his throat. "Well, anyone else wanting to stay here?"

Nova let out a sharp laugh. "Are you kidding? Winter's coming. This girl is going home."

Her comment broke the tension, making most of us chuckle. Raven returned to sit beside me while Embry took his place on the opposite side. I leaned close and whispered to her. "Thanks."

Raven shrugged nonchalantly, though I could see the dampness in her eyes. "What are friends for?"

While Embry filled his plate, I looked around the table and felt a wash of sadness. Yes, I knew this was the right move for me, but I would miss my family like crazy.

We can visit them whenever you wish, Embry sent to me. It startled me that he seemed to know what I'd been thinking. *And whenever you're ready to go home, I will happily follow.*

Thank you, I sent back, feeling my nerves settle at his words. Knowing this wasn't a long-term thing made the impending separation much easier. Once we all ate and some of my cousins went back to sleep, I found myself faced with Embry and Raven.

"I guess we should make sure Talon and Jade are okay with us staying here," I said to Raven, "but I don't want to disturb them on their first married morning."

"I'm sure it'll be fine," Raven said, waving this off. "We'll find them later this afternoon. Embry, when is the rest of your group heading back to California?"

"The ones that are will be heading back tomorrow," he said. "Jericho and Gerhard have both decided to stay in the area, Damien is traveling to New Zealand with Reya and Tristan, and Grey has found his family here, so he'll be staying as well."

"Sun Valley is about to have an influx of extremely good-looking residents," Raven said with a wink. "Well, I'll leave you two alone. I'm going to go tell Madeline the good news—and see if she can help us find jobs."

Raven had become close with Jade's mom during the wedding planning. I had a feeling that family dinners with the Callaghans were in our future. Spinning on her heel, Raven made her way to one of the sheds on the property, where she pulled out a bike to ride into town. I watched her go, then faced the man who would be my mate. "So, what now?"

"How about a walk?" Embry offered, holding his hand out, palm up.

"You'll leave your clothes on, right?" I murmured before accepting.

Heat moved through my body and settled in my cheeks. This man sure knew how to make me blush. He led me into the woods, and we walked together slowly, hand in hand. He seemed in no rush to get anywhere, and I felt the same. The sun had barely risen, and he paused to soak it in as a stream of light cut through the foliage.

"There were many years I was not able to do this. Walking through the darkness certainly makes you appreciate the light." His eyes opened and met mine, and I felt instantly sucked into his gaze. He had this crazy strong power over me that became more and more difficult to ignore.

Especially now, alone in the woods...

"Embry," I whispered huskily. We were so close I could feel his heat coming off him in waves. "Wait. Not—not yet. I mean, not that I didn't enjoy kissing you last night. I enjoyed it too much. But if we get wrapped up in the physical, I feel like we won't get to know each other the way we need to."

He stilled, his eyes continuing to search mine. For the moment, I couldn't breathe, couldn't speak. Couldn't look away from the tantalizing spell he weaved. When he finally answered, his voice remained calm. "All right. I understand how you feel. The physical connection between us is strong."

"Thank you," I said, feeling slightly dizzy. "I just—I feel overwhelmed by you."

"As I do by you." He smiled, two perfectly straight white rows of teeth. When he released me from his thrall, I stumbled into him. Steadying me with a light chuckle, he slipped his hand back down to mine and continued through the trees. "Let's keep moving before I do something I'll regret."

Chapter 2

Embry walked Valentina to her door after their hike through the woods. When they reached the porch, he turned to her with barely inches between them. "Could I see you this evening?"

"That would be nice. What time?"

"I'll pick you up at six o'clock if that would work." Valentina nodded before glancing around nervously. How did they part? A hug, another mind-numbing kiss? After he'd agreed to take the physical part slowly, Valentina didn't think he'd try that, but he was still a man....

Embry watched the play of emotions skitter across his mate's face with nothing short of amusement. Before she could wrap herself around a mental pole, Embry's hot hand grasped hers and brought it to his lips.

"Until then." And before he could change his mind, he turned and vanished, leaving Valentina staring after him. He had much to do before that night. He wanted everything to be perfect for his mate. For their first real date.

His first stop was the florist. He would order a beautiful bouquet for Valentina. Perhaps someone there could recommend a restaurant. Somewhere to go dancing or stargazing.

He was nervous, Embry realized. Wasn't that something? He couldn't remember any time in his life that he'd felt genuine nerves.

Stepping into the small floral shop, Embry perused the buckets of single-stemmed roses while the shop owner helped another customer. When that customer turned, she offered a bright smile. "Good morning! You were at the wedding, right? I'm Pearl, Jade's sister. We met, but I can't say I remember your name."

"Embry Jain, ma'am," he replied, bowing respectfully. Pearl giggled with delight.

"Such unfailing manners. What are you here for? Flowers for a special lady?"

"Very special."

"Anyone I know?

"Valentina Stone."

Pearl eyed him up and down; this must be the man that had Valentina so flustered at the rehearsal dinner. "First date? What do you have planned?"

"I—I'm not really sure yet."

"Oh, I'm so happy I had to drop off a check for Jade. You are in very capable hands, I assure you. Now, how are your cooking skills?"

"Non-existent, I'm afraid."

"That's just fine, we'll fix that. Terri? We need to help this fine gentleman pick out a bouquet for a very lucky lady."

Though Embry didn't fully understand what had happened, he suddenly found himself in a whirlwind of flowers, food, and music. After dragging him into several stores in town, Pearl handed him off to Emma's capable hands.

Jade's older sister had a calmer presence than Pearl. She wasn't as overly pushy as the mother of seven; her approach seemed to be more subtle. "Pearl said you're taking Valentina out tonight."

"That's the plan."

"How long have you known her?"

"We met just a few days ago."

"You live in two very different places. What are your plans?"

Embry looked into Emma's eyes, more serious than he'd ever been. "Valentina is the love of my life. I knew it the moment I met her. I will do anything to be with her."

"Oh, my," Emma said, patting her hand over her heart. "We better make sure tonight is absolutely perfect then. I assume you know how to peel and chop?"

"It might be all I know how to do when it comes to cooking."

"Good enough for today. Start with the potatoes, and we'll go from there." Emma patted down the steaks and gave them a generous amount of seasoning, setting them aside to work on a simple dough for biscuits. "What do you do for work?"

Embry didn't look away from his task when he answered. "Nothing consistent at the moment. We've been building homes for the homeless in California."

"Important work, but are you able to support yourself?"

"And Valentina, if she so wishes. I have...family money, and I enjoy working with charities."

Emma tilted her head as she studied him. "Where are you from?"

"I was born in Nepal, but it has been quite some time since I called it home."

"You did a lot of traveling before settling in California?"

"I did. Nowhere felt like home after losing my sister."

"Oh," Emma said, pausing in her work to place a hand over his. "I'm so sorry. I didn't know."

"It is not something I advertise, but thank you. It was a long time ago."

"That doesn't make it any easier. I couldn't imagine—" Emma shook her head sadly. "I understand why you've traveled so much. Too many memories?"

"Yes." Among other things.

Emma understood the need for a change in topic, so she asked, "How did you end up with the group you're with now?"

"We all work with the same charity," Embry said. They hadn't really discussed a backstory, but it seemed as good as any.

"It seems...strange."

"How so?"

"Jade never mentioned any of you, and then all of a sudden, you're all old friends and invited to her wedding. Plus, you're all— you know...." Emma gestured vaguely toward him, pink rising up her neck to settle into her cheeks.

Embry's eyebrows rose nearly to his hairline. "We're...?"

"Extremely good-looking. And none of you seem concerned with money. It just seems...."

"Strange," Embry finished for her.

"Exactly."

"Emma, there is nothing untoward happening here. We each have our own tale to tell, and we each feel we owe a debt to society. That is how we ended up in the same place and why we felt drawn to each other. We are brothers, not by blood but circumstance."

"That sounds nice and good, but I can't help but feel protective of Valentina."

"That is something we can agree on one hundred percent."

She studied him for a few moments more before jerking her head in a decisive nod. "As long as we understand each other."

"Now, tell me about you. When is the wedding date?"

"We decided on June," Emma said. "Rick and Cassie moved in not long after we got engaged, so there's been a bit of an adjustment, though not nearly as much as I thought there would be. Cassie loves Suzy and Mikey and vice-versa—it's like they've always been siblings."

"May I ask about their father?"

Emma watched her hands as she answered. "You know some of the story?"

"Jade told me what happened when he brought a gun into your home."

"It was the most horrible day of my life," Emma said, tears gathering in her eyes. "It still makes no sense to me, and I doubt it ever will, but he went through his court-mandated rehab and now he's serving three years for attempted murder."

"As difficult as it is, hopefully he will come out of it a changed man."

"He didn't put up a fuss when I asked for a divorce, but now he's been writing and asking to see the kids. I've put him off, but he's still their father. I'm not sure what to do."

"You will do what is right for you and your family."

She gave him half a smile. "If only it was that easy."

"Nothing in life ever is. Now, I have a mountain of potatoes here—what's the next step?"

"Dump them, carefully, into that pot of boiling water. The dough needs some time to rise, and we don't want to cook the steaks until it's almost time, so all that's left is snapping beans."

Embry secured the lid on the pot of potatoes and started in with the beans. They worked in companionable silence for a few minutes before he caught Emma smiling at him. "What?"

"You're a good listener and very easy to talk to. Valentina is a lucky girl."

"Kind of you to say."

As buns baked and the first steaks were laid on the grill, Rick led the three children into the house and they immediately ran to Emma for hugs. It was a happy picture and one Embry found himself longing for. Rick shook Embry's hand. "That smells great."

"Good, because we have enough for all of you and my date and possibly an army if there is one marching through."

"Thankfully not, but we'll enjoy it all the same."

"I appreciate Emma's help with this and you letting me borrow her expertise."

"Anytime. Good luck tonight."

"With this meal, he won't need it," Emma said, handing over carefully packed dishes. "Have fun, and tell Valentina I said I approve."

Embry found himself chuckling as he left, and he couldn't remember the last time that sound had passed his lips. Taking the image of the happy family with him, Embry left to get dressed for his first date with his mate.

Chapter 3

Blowing out a breath, I entered the house to talk to my best friend. Finding Raven draped sideways over a large, overstuffed chair in the living room, headphones on and feet bobbing in time to whatever music she listened to, I took a moment to study her. Since her eyes were closed, I approached with caution, not wanting to scare her.

"Raven!" I called out, forcing her eyes open.

"Hey!" she yelled back, louder than intended with the music still blaring. Taking them off with a sheepish grin, she said, "Oops, sorry. How's it going?"

"Good."

"Good? That's all I get? Come on, girl, dish!"

Chuckling, I plopped down on the couch and craned my neck to look up the stairs. "My brother isn't here, is he?"

"No. Once they all took a nap, Pearl dropped by and offered a tour of the next town over. They all went to shop for souvenirs."

"Okay, good." I sighed. "Ugh, Raven, I don't know what I'm doing."

"Well, it's not like either of us has much dating experience."

"True, but it's so much more than that. Embry is...overwhelming. He takes over my whole body and brain."

"Really," Raven purred, dragging out the single word. "Tell me more."

Throwing a pillow at her head, I groaned. "Not like that. Well, not yet. Oh my God, I can't even imagine what *that* will be like! I asked him if we could wait on anything...physical."

"Good move," she said with an approving nod. "He'll probably be so good in bed you'll just become a mindless sex slave."

"Raven!" I squealed, color darkening my cheeks again. It seemed to be a recurring event around here.

She shrugged. "What? I only speak the truth."

"Just wait. You'll probably have a mate out there, too. And then it'll be payback time."

"Ha! Show me the man that could handle all of this," she said, making a sweeping motion to encompass herself. "No mere mortal—or Elemental, for that matter—could tame me."

Shaking my head at her antics, I said, "Okay, new subject. What happened with Madeline?"

"Oh! She's so awesome. She said we could help out at their real estate firm for now—it'll only be part-time, but it's something. And we're invited to dinner on Sunday. I may have mentioned your interest in Embry, so he's invited, too."

Called it. "Great. Don't you remember Lani's stories about Jade's family?"

"Well, at least this way, they won't be trying to set you up with anyone else," Raven reasoned. "God only knows who they'll find for me."

"None of the Elementals at the wedding did it for you?" I asked, more seriously this time, curious about her answer.

"No. Maybe I'm just not built for a mate."

At this I had to laugh. "If I am, then you certainly are."

Shrugging again, Raven stood and smoothed down her shirt. "Why don't we go see if Talon and Jade are done making googly eyes at each other?"

"Sounds good," I said, collecting my purse and following her out.

Though we'd rented a couple of cars for our stay—and Talon had generously offered the use of his—Raven and I opted to ride the bikes. Besides the fact that it took less than ten minutes to get anywhere in town, the crisp autumn day seemed best enjoyed without the confines of doors.

As we neared Talon's drive, we could hear the delighted squeals of children.

"I wonder who's here," I commented, though I didn't expect a response. As we rounded the final bend, I recognized most of Pearl's kids running around in the yard.

Raven and I slowed and endured several rounds of hugs. The youngest five were here—Ewan, Ella, Kalia, Hazel, and Perrin.

When I'd first met the twins, I'd immediately felt a connection to them. Lani and Samson confirmed that these two were Gifted—the only ones in the family, much like Jade had been the only one in hers. It made me wonder how that worked—why my whole extended family seemed to carry the gene, while these kids—who obviously had Gifted on both sides of the family—didn't.

"Valentina, Raven!" Jade called out from across the yard. She and Talon had been relaxing at a small table. "How are you?"

"Great!" I said, hauling Hazel up on a hip while Raven lifted Perrin. Though they weren't quite a year old, they were certainly advanced for their age. They were already running with their older siblings. As we approached the table, I raised an eyebrow at Jade. "Pearl got you to babysit on your honeymoon?"

Jade grinned. "I guess it's practice. You ready for two of these, honey?"

Talon couldn't stop the proud beam if he had wanted to. "Of course."

Rolling her eyes at us, Jade reached over to clasp Talon's hand. "What's up with you guys?"

"Actually," I began, "I've decided to stay. We've decided to stay. We were hoping we could live in one of your places?"

"Sure," Talon agreed immediately. "Would you like to stay in the house you are now?"

"Yes!" Raven and I replied simultaneously.

Talon and Jade chuckled. "That's no problem. There are also a few from California who have decided to stay. We told them they can use the property at Black Bear Lake as long as they'd like."

Clearing my throat, I decided to get everything out in the open. "We heard about that...from Embry."

"Oh?" Jade asked, a twinkle in her eye. Was I that obvious?

"Yeah. Turns out, we're...mates," I finished, wanting to disappear into the ground.

"I thought I saw some sparks between you two last night," Jade said with a wink.

"Your mom has already helped us find work," Raven piped in. "Oh, and we'll see you at dinner on Sunday."

"Be prepared for a madhouse," Jade said. "I'm really glad you're staying a little longer. With the craziness this week, I feel like I didn't get to spend much time with you."

"Don't worry," I said. "In no time, you'll be sick of us."

∞ ∞ ∞

MY BREATH CAME IN SHORT little gasps, my heart beating out a dance club tempo. If there had been a paper bag in sight, I would have snatched it to try that whole breathing-into-a-bag thing.

"Valentina, Embry's at the door..." Raven announced with a cursory knock before entering my room.

I turned to her with wide eyes, wearing nothing but a slip. I'd wanted to dress nice for the date, but there was an issue with that. Much to my humiliation, I spoke with a suspiciously girly whine. "I have nothing to wear."

"Oh, sweetie, it's all right." Raven instantly ran to my side, soothing me with her gentle voice.

"This is ridiculous," I said with a forced laugh. "What is wrong with me?"

"Nothing, sweetheart. You're a girl. This is what we do."

"I don't. Ugh, please help me."

Raven took both my hands and looked into my eyes. "You're lucky I barged in here. Come with me." She led me out of the room and down the hall, pushing open Tayen's door. "She'll be right down!" she called out to Embry on the way past the stairs.

Humiliation swamped me again as I realized he could hear everything we were saying. Panic rose and nearly crippled me. *You're not listening to us, are you?*

Of course not, though I can feel your anxiety. Is everything all right?

His soothing voice did a lot to calm my jumping nerves. *It will be. I'll be right down...and keep your ears to yourself.*

Embry's laughter floated across my mind, igniting my nerve endings in a whole new way.

Raven wholly focused on her task, sorting through the closet of my brother's room, pushing aside the suit he'd worn to the wedding to get her hands on Tayen's clothes. Of the three of us, she definitely had the most fashion sense—and luckily for Raven and me, we were all about the same size.

"Ah! Perfect," Raven said with a grin, snatching out a dress and shoving it into my hands. "Put this on while I find her shoe stash."

"Good thing they aren't leaving until tomorrow," I murmured, doing as Raven told me.

The dress had long, flowy lines, a dark blue with a pretty flower pattern. I put it on like one would a robe, using the ties at the waist to hold it together. There were sleeves to the elbow, but a low V-neckline and when I walked, most of my leg showed through the slit. While it was undeniably beautiful, I suddenly felt extremely self-conscious. "Raven, I'm not sure about this..."

She shooed the thought away with a wave of her hand. "You'll forget that as soon as Embry gets a load of you. Here, put these on."

Shoving a pair of shoes into my hands, she sat me on the edge of the bed and climbed up behind me, pulling my long hair back into a loose braid. While she did that I clasped on a pair of nude heels, which had a strap high around the ankle. Once the shoes were on, she came around to the front to check my make-up.

"You just need a little eyeliner," she decided, digging through Tayen's collection on the side table. She came back and pulled my lid down, applying the liner with the ease of long practice. "There! All done."

With a deep breath I stood, slightly wobbly in the shoes. Tayen wore a size up from me, and I didn't wear heels often. But when I mentioned tennis shoes to Raven, her look alone told me how dumb they would look with the dress.

"Thanks," I said to my best friend. "I think I would have just canceled without your help."

"That's what I'm here for. Now, go get 'em," she said with a wink before shoving me out the door.

Taking slow steps back to the stairs, I gripped the rail and concentrated on not falling down them. By the time I hit the last stair and finally looked up, I realized Embry had been staring at me.

He wore black dress pants, a dark blue button-down, and a matching black vest. I paused in my movements, my gaze drifting down to his toes and back up again, swallowing to help my unexpectedly dry throat.

Embry had yet to utter a word, and I began to grow anxious again. This was all a mistake. I should go back upstairs, put on something comfortable...

"You are stunning," he finally said, his voice slightly deeper than normal. Reaching out to grasp my hand, he placed his hot lips against my skin, sending tingles down my spine. "I am the luckiest man in the world."

A smile lit my face, fire racing into my cheeks once again. Raven had been right—I'd forgotten my self-consciousness as soon as Embry spoke.

"You look rather dashing yourself," I said, then wondered where those words had come from. I'd never used *dashing* in my life. "I mean, you look...good."

I prefer dashing, he said on our private link, a spark lighting in his eye.

You would, I sent back with a smirk. Aloud, I asked, "Shall we?"

He led the way out the door, wrapping my hand through the crook of his arm. In the driveway sat a Porsche—one of Talon's collection. "Talon loaned me the vehicle for tonight," Embry said as he opened the passenger door. It had to be the nicest car I'd ever been in. "I wanted the best for you."

I sat and twirled my legs inside before answering. "That's really sweet, but I'm a down to earth kind of girl. I don't need a lot of pomp."

Embry leaned down, his face just inches from mine. "That doesn't mean you don't deserve it," he whispered, moving closer yet to brush his lips against my cheek. My heart began racing again, and he knew perfectly well his effect on me. He moved around to the driver's side as I tried to calm my breathing, but I had a feeling I'd just gotten a preview of the night's events.

"Where are we going?" I asked as he put the car in gear.

"That's a surprise. Let me take care of you tonight. Will you let me do that?"

I made the mistake of looking into his eyes. Unable to speak, I did the unthinkable. With a simple nod, I put my life into his very capable hands.

Chapter 4

Embry drove through town, stopping in a small park on the outskirts. He got out and sped around to open my door, offering his hand as I stood. So far, this hadn't been what I'd expected.

"We have a little way to walk. Will you be comfortable enough in those shoes?"

"Is there a path?"

"There is."

"I should be fine," I said, though I didn't quite believe it myself. Walking in heels on solid ground presented enough dilemmas, but I'd do my best.

We followed the path together, his hand on the small of my back effectively warding off the chill in the air. After several minutes I spotted a strange glow in the air as we came to a small clearing. When we reached the edge, I stared in amazement, taking in the bistro table set for two, the strings of twinkly lights lending the entire area an otherworldly effect, and the bouquet of roses placed on my chair.

"Embry, this is beautiful," I whispered, afraid of speaking too loudly and ruining the moment.

"I'm glad you approve." He smiled. "Jade's sister helped me with the meal."

"You cooked?" I asked, craning my neck up to look at him in surprise.

His smile turned sheepish as he admitted, "I mostly watched. But I did do most of the chopping. Knife skills are one thing I do possess."

"Well, I appreciate the attempt." I chuckled, letting him lead me into the clearing and sliding into the seat he held out for me. "Which sister was it?"

"Emma," Embry replied. "Rick happily took the children to the park for the afternoon after Pearl told him he had to."

"I'll have to thank them both later, then," I said, spreading a napkin on my lap. Though the evening carried a cool breeze, I stayed nice and warm. "Are you controlling the temperature somehow?"

He pointed one lithe finger along the ground, where I could see a thin trail of rock salt in a loose circle. "I have created our own little bubble."

Both eyebrows raised now as I looked back at him with awe. "That's a neat trick."

"With all the powers Elementals are granted, it is only our own imagination that limits us. Ever since I have been given a second chance, I have vowed each and every day not to waste it."

"Do you think you'll ever forgive yourself?" I asked, then bit my lip. "I'm sorry, that probably wasn't the best thing to ask."

Embry reached across the table to grip my hand in his. With his eyes boring into mine, he answered, "Never believe there is a question you cannot ask. I will always be honest with you, Valentina. There cannot be an untruth between mates. However, there are some things from my past that I wouldn't want to burden you with. They may also make you think less of me."

His face turned downcast, and it was my turn to bolster him. "Embry, no matter what you've done, it doesn't change who you are now. If this mate thing is true, then I'm going to want to know all of it. Maybe not right away, or all at once, but I want to know everything about you. Just like I hope you'll want to learn everything about me."

"You are the most incredible woman," Embry murmured, his eyes clearing of his shadowed past. "I will live every day just in amazement that the universe has chosen you for me to spend my days with."

My heart fluttering in my chest, I tried to come up with something to do or say. Soft music played, though I couldn't pinpoint from where. An idea struck. Standing, I held out both hands for his. "Dance with me."

His slow smile melted my insides. "It would be my pleasure."

Embry wrapped me in his arms, holding me closer than he had during our dance at the wedding. Resting my head against his chest, I listened to the steady beat of his heart, using it as my guide as he twirled me gently along the ground.

It became difficult to ignore how our bodies fit so perfectly together, even though he had several inches of height on me, and his shoulders were twice as wide as my own. I managed to find the perfect niche against his frame, his sheer strength making me feel small and delicate.

Feminine.

It was a wonderful feeling, and one I savored even as our dance came to a close. Embry leaned back and raised my chin with two fingers to gaze into my eyes. "Hungry?"

"Starved. I can't wait to try what you've made." I sat again as Embry unveiled the product of his afternoon's labor; a pile of mashed potatoes stacked with green beans and a perfectly grilled steak on top, drizzled with a red wine sauce. He also revealed a basket of homemade biscuits, with fresh herbs pressed into the tops.

"Wow, this looks amazing."

"Thank you," he replied, pouring each of us a glass of wine. "Tell me more about yourself."

"What would you like to know?"

"Everything—but let's start with what you like to do for fun."

Pondering that for a moment, I took a roll, broke it in half. Steam escaped, and I marveled over how he managed that, too. "Raven and I like going to concerts. We'd road trip up to Albuquerque to see some bigger names, but we both preferred this little place in Las Cruces where we could see up and coming local bands. I had a job waitressing while I went to school, but I haven't really decided yet what I want to do with my life. What do you do?"

"For fun, or for work?"

"Both, I guess. Living as long as you have, you must have done many things."

"I was born in a small village of Nepal. My sister and I loved to explore the area, and I find being outdoors is still one of my favorite things."

"Your sister? Is she your twin?"

"Yes. Her name is—was Rika."

"I'm sorry," I said instantly, reaching over to grasp his hand. "You don't have to talk about her if you don't want."

"No, it's fine. I wish for you to know. Rika and I were inseparable for many years, traveling to new places but always going back to our home. In the late seventeen-hundreds, we lost our parents in the war between Nepal and China. Rika and I fled, and I haven't returned since."

"Where did you go?"

"Across Europe. Romania, Italy. We couldn't stay anywhere for long; ten or fifteen years and we'd start to be questioned on our appearance. Eventually we ended up in Spain, and then we caught a ship to the new world.

"The journey was difficult since we couldn't use our powers in front of the humans. We hit a storm, and the ship sank. Rika and I did our best to save as many as possible, but by the time the chaos ended—she was nowhere to be found."

"Oh, Embry," I murmured, unsure what to do or say.

"We lost our psychic connection, and I believed she was gone. For many years I wandered America, hiding in the mountains and severely limiting my interactions with people. That's when I met Ferghus."

My eyebrows drew together as I asked, "The daemon?"

"At first, I believed him to be an Elemental, like me. We spoke at length over the next few years, and he told me of a world full of power. A world where I could get my sister back." Embry's tortured gaze lifted, met mine. The full impact of his words floored me.

"You mean...he convinced you Rika could be resurrected?"

"He did. I was grieving, Valentina. I would have done anything to have my family back. So, I joined Ferghus, not realizing the seed of darkness had already taken over. He promised me exactly what I wanted to hear, and I fell for it. Hook, line, and sinker."

"He lied to you. Turned you into a shadowman," I said, barely above a whisper.

"He did, yet he did not. It was my decisions that led me to that fate, and I take full responsibility. By the time I realized what Ferghus had gotten me into, it was too late. My soul was shadowed, and I didn't want to return to my old ways."

Embry looked so torn up, so tormented. Without thinking I stood, walked over and sat on his lap. Placing both palms against his cheeks, I forced him to look me in the eye. "I'm sorry for what you went through. I can't imagine what I'd be like if I ever lost my brother. You are stronger than you know, and you've been given a chance to start over."

"How can you still look at me, knowing what you know now?"

"What I know now is that you're a good man who grieved the loss of his sister. You were vulnerable, and this Ferghus took advantage of that. I know you regret things you've done, but you can't take them back. You can only do better. That's the man I'm looking at now."

To prove my words, I pressed my lips firmly against his. At first he didn't respond, but I only became more insistent. The moment I felt him give in, his hands gripped my waist and his tongue swept across the seam of my lips. Opening to him willingly, I met him kiss for kiss, passion for passion. Though the kiss ignited every one of my nerve endings, it was meant to soothe, to comfort.

When he pulled away, we both gasped for breath. His hands slid from my waist to my back, pressing me gently against his chest. I snuggled into him, realizing he needed a moment to come to grips with his emotions.

"Thank you," he finally murmured against the top of my head.

Pulling away, I smiled softly. "You're very welcome. Now, I only have one more question."

"What's that?"

"Is there dessert?"

<h1 style="text-align:center">Chapter 5</h1>

Saying goodbye to my family proved even more difficult than I'd imagined. Raven and I drove with them to Duluth, even though it was a little over an hour away. We watched them walk through security at the small airport, waving with tears in our eyes until we could no longer see them.

As we walked back to our borrowed car with low spirits, Raven perked up just a little. "Let's spend a little time here. We can get lunch, go shopping."

"All right," I said, still feeling a heaviness in my heart. "Any idea where to go?"

"Pearl told me about some cute shops downtown; I say we start there. We're going to need some warmer clothes, at the very least."

"That's a good point," I conceded. "My two sweatshirts definitely won't hack it much longer."

We navigated away from the airport and made a pit stop at the mall we happened to pass on our way back to the steep hill that led to the downtown area. Raven and I both found winter coats and a few other items to pad our wardrobe before continuing on our adventure.

As we started downhill, the view of Lake Superior nearly took our breath away. "I wonder if the people living here ever get used to this view."

"I'm not sure I would. It's like living on the ocean," Raven replied. "And right now, with the fall colors—man, I wouldn't mind seeing this every day."

"I'm sure we can visit Reese and Arie anytime."

"Can I tell you a secret? Emerson and Dominic scare me a little."

"Really?" I asked, surprised. Nothing seemed to scare Raven. "Why?"

"They're just so...serious all the time. Plus, that thing Emerson can do—I guess I don't want to get too cozy."

"They're good guys, though. Just over-protective. I'd like to meet Edith and Anya. They have such heartbreaking stories."

"I would, too. We'll set up a time with Reese in the next couple of weeks. Give them a little time to get settled."

"Arie's brother is pretty cute," I said, just to niggle Raven a bit. "Are you sure he doesn't do anything for you?"

"Oh, I'm sure. Besides, he's already got a mate."

"What?"

"You didn't notice? He's meant to be with Reya's daughter."

"What!" This time I screeched the word. "But she's a *baby*."

Raven shrugged. "In this world, that doesn't really matter, does it? She'll grow up, and Aden will stay the same."

"Still, though. That's kinda gross."

"Think about this. When you were born, Embry was already centuries old. How is that different?"

She had a point there. "Because we didn't meet until I was an adult."

"Aden doesn't have any untoward feelings for Leia. He protects her like an older brother. Maybe having him live away from her for a while will be a good thing."

"Must be difficult for them both, though," I murmured. I'd only just met Embry, and I couldn't imagine being away from him for any amount of time. Even our little day trip today—I found myself constantly reaching out, sometimes speaking on our private link, sometimes just feeling him there.

"What is it?" Raven asked, reading me like a book.

"This whole mate thing. It's weird, Raven. And wonderful. And scary."

"How do you mean?"

"I barely know Embry, but I can't imagine being apart. Even these last few hours, I find myself needing to speak to him. To know he's okay."

"Sounds like obsession."

"Feels like it, too. How am I supposed to know what I'm feeling isn't just a crazy amount of lust? I've never been attracted to a man before. What if I'm just reacting to the physical?"

"Can you have a real conversation with him?"

Our date last night flitted through my mind. "Yes."

"Does he listen to you and respond appropriately?"

"Yes."

"Well, that's a good start."

"Promise me something?"

"Anything."

"If at any point you think I'm acting on lust alone, just hit me over the head or something, okay? Call me out on it."

"You got it," Raven promised.

∞ ∞ ∞

WHEN WE ARRIVED BACK TO our cabin, Raven and I both changed into new outfits—a comfortable pair of jeans for me, with a pale gold silk shirt Raven assured me matched my skin and brought out the lightness in my eyes—and donned our new jackets before deciding to return the car we'd borrowed from Jade.

You have arrived back safely?

We have, I answered Embry. *Heading to Jade's now to return her car. What are you up to?*

That's perfect. I am also at Jade's, saying goodbye to the men heading back to California. I would like to introduce you, officially.

I began to hyperventilate, and Raven noticed. "What's wrong?"

Wide eyes shot to her. "He wants me to meet the California Elementals."

"So?"

"So? They're like his family. Big, scary, good-looking family."

Raven chuckled as she maneuvered the streets. "You'll be fine."

Valentina? Is everything all right?

Taking deep breaths, I managed to calm myself enough to answer without panic obvious in my tone. *I'm fine. We'll be there shortly.*

When we arrived, we found a rather large crowd gathered in Talon and Jade's backyard. Though I'd seen all the Elementals at the wedding, I hadn't been introduced to most of them. That would change now.

Embry appeared beside my door as soon as we parked. He opened it and offered his hand to assist me out of the car. To my amusement, another Elemental did the same for Raven.

"Thank you," I said, squeezing my free hand in a fist to hide my nerves.

Embry leaned down to place a sweet kiss on my cheek. *You look beautiful.*

A blush crept up my neck, and I felt even more hesitant to meet his friends—his brothers. We walked hand in hand and as we approached the group, suddenly all eyes were on us. "Everyone, please meet Valentina Stone. My mate."

I forgot how to speak. Frozen to the spot, I simply waited to be swallowed whole.

Raven arrived at my side and gripped my shaking hand. "And I'm Raven Blackfoot. It's nice to meet you all."

The group continued to stare, and I could feel my heart beating so hard I was surprised it didn't simply leap out of my chest. Someone had to do something, say something. Anything.

Luckily, a man with strange, aqua eyes approached first, effectively hiding me from view. "Valentina, a pleasure. I am Damien Nikora."

He's the one you told me about? The seer?

That's correct.

"Pleased to meet you," I said aloud.

Then, one by one, the former shadowmen introduced themselves, shook my hand. They were treating me with something akin to deference, and I found myself unnerved by their unfailing manners.

Why are they acting so strange toward me?

Not strange. I am the first of our group to find my mate. After so many years of darkness, sorrow, you are like a shining beacon of hope. That perhaps they, too, may have been redeemed enough to earn something so precious as you.

His words floored me and forced me to see these men in a new light. Suddenly, my nerves dissipated, and I put genuine feeling into my introductions. I also tried to remember each of their names.

Lucius Nicolette, his Greek roots evident in his dark, nearly black hair and deep teal eyes. Augustus Lawrence, a slight British accent telling me his origins, studying me with light, hazel eyes. His long, dark brown hair secured at the nape of his neck reminded me of a gentleman from an earlier century. Silas O'Toole, an Irish accent very much in evidence, with buzzed, light brown hair and soft blue eyes.

I'd heard the story of Kate saving these three, and their unusually close relationship that helped them fight the darkness for longer than any of them could have done on their own. They were also part of the group heading to Ireland.

Next came Jericho Winther, who had decided to stay in the area. Gerhard Holmes, a man Embry had told me was also staying, seemed to be absent.

Grey Elliot—also staying in the area, with the discovery of his relation to Pearl's husband—introduced himself next, along with Amal Klimek, Devidas Pompei, Ravi Hertz, Ivan Hurst, and Dimitri Zavala. They all had been shadowed but were now returned to the light.

Finally, Frances Borg approached to say hello. He hadn't been part of the California group but had been the first of the shadowmen to be saved by Jade. Though we'd met several months ago in Mescalero, now, as he walked forward, a vision superimposed itself upon the one I currently saw.

Frances, approaching me as he did now. A beautiful blonde woman at his side, her smile wide. She wore a glittering gown that rivaled a queen. He wore an outfit very different from the jeans and polo he sported now—gold brocade-lined pants and a stiff, starchy jacket with tassels. On his head sat a crown.

I blinked, and the vision disappeared. His smile faltered at the look on my face, so I shook the image away and took his hand. "Nice to see you."

"Everything all right?" he asked.

"Just fine," I said, forcing myself to smile.

Tristan and Reya arrived then, so the question I could see in Frances' eyes didn't have the opportunity to be asked. Samson and Lani weren't too far behind, along with Malakai Scott and his family, plus Jared, Hugh, and Kate.

Using the diversion as an opportunity to speak with Reya, I promised Embry and Raven I'd return and snuck through the crowd to her side.

Chapter 6

When I reached Reya, I gently pulled her aside. "May I speak with you, privately?"

"Of course. Let's go inside." We slipped through the back door and entered the drool-worthy kitchen that Talon had painstakingly remodeled. The entire home looked gorgeous, seamlessly blending Talon's Native roots with Jade's own personal style. I hoped one day I'd have a house like this. "Is everything okay?"

"Oh, yes," I said, realizing she probably thought I needed a doctor. "I was just hoping to speak with you about your...ability."

"Which one?" she asked with half a smile.

"The way you...foresee certain things."

"Oh." Her eyebrows knit as she thought through her answer. "That one's relatively new. What would you like to know?"

"How does it work?"

She leaned back against a counter, resting one elbow in her palm and propping her chin on her free hand. "Well, so far, my visions have come to me in dreams. The visions themselves are not very clear, and I'm still learning to understand the message in them."

"What do you mean?"

"Like with Lani—I had a dream I was lost in the desert, and I knew something was wrong. Then a woman appeared, covered in blood, and she said, 'help me.' Though I'd never seen Lani before, I knew it was her, and obviously that she would need help. I didn't know when or where, except that it would be in a desert."

"Lani had that same vision in the divining pool, right?" Reya nodded. "Is that how it always works?"

"I believe it comes out different in every person. Why do you ask?"

Sucking in a deep breath, I braced my own palms on the counter behind me. Though I'd told Lani—and, subsequently, most of the reservation—about my ability back when the daemons attacked, it still felt strange to talk about something I'd hidden for so long. "I—I have a similar ability."

"That's wonderful," Reya said with a smile.

"I'm not so sure."

"What do you mean?" she asked, her head cocking to the side.

"They've never been helpful, for one. I just see a possible future in the place I'm in, or for a person I'm looking at."

"Can you give me an example?"

I looked toward the backyard. "Just now, when Frances walked toward me to say hi, I saw him dressed...differently. Like a king. And he wore a crown. He was walking toward me the same way he did outside, except he was smiling, and we were definitely not in Wisconsin. A blonde woman walked beside him, like they were both greeting me."

"Like a mate?"

"Possibly," I said. "That one was unusual. Normally I see different people or things in the place I am, not the other way around. Like I'll walk into my mom's living room in the middle of May and see Christmas decorations, and when December comes, it'll look exactly the same. Or when I was waitressing, I'd walk up to a table and see a different group sitting there, and they'd show up the next day. Things like that."

"Interesting. I'd love to have Damien join us for this conversation—would you mind?"

"I guess not. It's strange for me to talk about this—growing up, only Josiah and Raven knew. Most of the tribe now knows, out of necessity. But I haven't talked about it with anyone else."

"Not even Embry?" I shook my head, but Reya didn't chastise me. "We'll keep it to ourselves."

The door opened, and the man with the aqua eyes and dark hair joined us. Reya must have asked Tristan to send him in. "How can I help?" he asked, perfectly polite.

After I explained my ability, Damien listened carefully before asking more specific questions. "Have you ever forced a vision?"

"No," I said. "I didn't ever think about it."

"I'd like you to try that now."

"How?"

"May I?" he asked, holding his hands out. Unsure but willing to try, I placed my palms against his. His fingers wrapped around mine, snug but not too tight. "Pick one thing. This counter, the fridge. Anything that catches your eye."

I looked around and chose the coffee maker. "All right."

"Good. Now, as you look at it, relax your mind. Open yourself up to your gift. Allow it to come to you."

I stared hard at the coffee maker, but nothing happened. "I'm not sure I'm doing this right."

"It's all right. This is new and unfamiliar. Try again. Focus, and listen to my voice. You are standing in the desert. The sun is high in the sky, warming your skin. A single cactus stands before you. It is springtime, and the color has become dark green from the rains. A small flower blooms, bright pink. You can smell the aftermath of rain—swollen earth, sweet creosote, gentle sage."

As he spoke, I did my best to force all thoughts away and only focus on his words. He painted a picture that became clear as day. I closed my eyes and breathed in the scent of home. When my eyes opened again, I saw Jade filling the coffee pot with water.

"I remember when I didn't even drink this stuff."

Talon approached from behind, hugged her around her stomach. "They're a lot to keep up with, that's for sure."

Jade closed her eyes and leaned back into him. "We have a little bit before they wake up."

"I can think of a few ways to keep ourselves entertained." Talon smiled and kissed her neck.

As she turned into his arms, a wail rose from upstairs, followed by another. Jade groaned and placed her forehead against Talon's shoulder. "That's Ember and Terran. The girls will be next."

"Get your coffee, my love. I'll get the boys."

Stumbling back, I blinked several times to bring the here and now back into focus. Damien watched me carefully, patiently. Reya gripped my arm and felt my forehead. "Are you all right?"

"Yeah, fine," I breathed, looking from the coffee maker to the hall, as if expecting to see Talon come down the stairs with children in hand. "That worked."

"Tell us everything," Damien insisted.

I did, with as much detail as I could recall. "It was different than any other vision I've had. I've never heard a conversation before, I would always just see a scene."

Continuing with my description, I watched Reya grin when she heard the boys' names, then even wider at the next piece of news. "They're going to have twin girls, too."

"If my vision is right," I said.

"Don't doubt yourself. You have amazing power, you only need to practice to bring it out."

Nodding, I managed a smile. "Thank you. That was pretty amazing."

"Anytime. I only wish we were staying longer; I would love to work with both you and Reya."

"Thanks. Maybe I'll come visit New Zealand. I've always wanted to travel abroad."

"Anytime," Reya assured me. Her head cocked, and a strange look came over her face. "We should get back outside. Something's happening."

The three of us rushed outside, and I took a moment to observe the scene before me. Malakai's young son, Daku, had the rapt attention of every person standing in the yard. My gaze traveled unerringly to Embry, who sought me out at the same time.

As I rushed to his side, he spoke into my mind. *Is everything all right?*

Just fine. What's going on?

"Daku, would you repeat that?" Tristan asked, wrapping his arm around Reya's shoulder as she reached his side.

The young man swallowed nervously, taking in the crowd surrounding him. I didn't know much about Malakai and his family; he had helped Reya and Tristan, and they lived in Australia. He'd officiated Reya and Tristan's wedding ceremony, along with Jade and Talon's. Magic ran in their family, though it differed from the Elemental magic.

"As many of you know, I have completed my koradji training. Like my father, and his father before him, I have been blessed with the visions. As I sleep, my spirit travels." He looked to Reya, and she nodded in encouragement. I knew Reya had a similar gift—as a daughter of a male foreseer, she had both the gifts of her parents, along with her own healing powers. "For many moons now, I have been in contact with a woman who needs help. She refuses to speak with me, even in her dreams."

"Do you know her name? Anything about her?" Damien asked.

"Only what she looks like, and that she is haunted by terrible things."

Jade spoke up this time. "Daku, I have some artistic ability. I could try sketching her if you would describe her to me."

"Someone needs to help this woman," Lucius said.

Daku suddenly looked nervous, bordering on frightened. Jade smiled gently at him, then at the crowd gathered. "Daku and I will work on a sketch. We'll go from there."

I noticed she touched his arm, and his face cleared of the anxiety. As an empath, Jade had a difficult time leaving anyone in distress. I turned to Embry. "I'd like to go inside with them. Will you be all right out here?"

"Of course."

Raven came with, joined by Reya, Kate, and Lani. Hopefully a group of women wouldn't overwhelm Daku.

Jade led the way upstairs, to the room she'd converted into her photography studio. She kept other art supplies in there but before I could follow the rest of the group, Raven held me back. "What's going on with you?"

"What do you mean?"

She raised an eyebrow, and I immediately hunched in on myself. "I spoke to Reya and Damien about...what I can do."

"Really? Could they help?"

"Actually, yes. Damien helped me force a vision. It was pretty incredible—I saw..." Realizing Jade was just in the next room, I shook my head and said instead, "I'll tell you more about it later."

Though her lips pursed, Raven nodded in agreement. We walked into the room where Jade had settled in a chair, her sketchbook in hand.

While they worked, I edged around the women gathered until I got a clear view of Daku. After my success with the vision downstairs, I thought I'd try something while he described this mystery woman to Jade.

Staring at the young, handsome man with deep, copper skin and the prettiest honey eyes framed by enviously long lashes, I forced my body to relax and my mind to clear. Using Damien's imagery from earlier, I focused on a picture of a cactus in bloom. Smelled the scent of the desert. Closed my eyes, took a deep breath. And opened them.

Daku sat, much as he did now. He'd grown a little taller, filled out a little more. Strong jaw, black hair long enough to tie at the base of his neck. No longer a young man, he was simply a man.

Beside him sat a woman. Long, wavy dark hair fell around her shoulders as she reached down to pick something off the ground. Daku rested a casual hand against her back, his lips curving into a smile as she looked up at him. Love shimmered between them, bright as the north star.

The woman turned her head, intense gray eyes locking on me. I recognized that look. Those eyes.

I stumbled back with a gasp, nearly landing on my backside. Luckily, Raven caught me before I could make a complete fool of myself. All eyes in the room looked at me, and I stared down at the half-completed drawing in Jade's hands.

Embry, you need to come in here.

Seconds later, Embry had replaced Raven at my side. His arm wrapped around my back, and on taking in my pale features, he placed a palm against my cheek. "What's happened?"

"Embry...look."

He turned, zeroed in on what I pointed at. And there, staring back at him with such similar eyes, was his sister. Stunned, his voice was no more than a whisper. "Rika."

"You know her?" Daku demanded—clearly protective of the woman in the picture.

"That's...that's my sister."

All the women in the room exchanged glances, but Embry and Daku took no notice. "Where is she? How can we find her?" Daku asked.

"I...I don't know. I thought I lost her, many years ago."

"You *lost* her?" Daku stood now, faced off with Embry. The shock of his actions left us all immobile. "What kind of brother are you?"

"Hey!" I yelled out. "Back off!"

He instantly shrank back, then looked sheepishly up at Embry. "I apologize."

With a stiff nod, Embry walked over to Jade and held his hand out for the sketchpad. Lifting it gingerly, he ran a finger over her hair. "She always loved her hair. Refused to cut it shorter or even braid it. She wanted it to be wild and free."

His eyes met mine, and the emotion swirling in those gray depths nearly undid me. "Embry, she's alive. We'll find her."

"You're not able to speak to her?" Reya asked.

"No," Embry said. "We were separated long ago. Our psychic connection went blank. I always hoped she lived, but I spent years searching and couldn't find her. Any trace of her. I'd given up."

"It's happened before. Tristan and Lani spent a century apart. Hugh and Jared lost connection when Hugh had amnesia. Even Dominic and Emerson couldn't connect when Arie held Emerson with a spell."

Embry spun on Reya, a fire in his eyes I didn't recognize. "You think she's being held hostage?"

Tristan appeared at Reya's side, his stance on instant guard. "I'll ask you not to speak to my mate that way."

Talon arrived next, worried for Jade and their babies. The tension in the room could have been cut with a knife. We all held our breath, waiting for it to break—or for a fight to happen.

Jade stepped between us all, ignoring Talon's restraining arm, and held her hands out. "All right, it's getting a little crowded in here. Everyone take a breath, relax. Let's go downstairs and discuss this rationally."

For a moment, no one moved. With a hesitant, *Embry?* he finally gave in.

His gaze met mine, softened. The scary red haze receded, and he came back to my side. "If my sister is alive, I will do everything in my power to find her. Daku, I appreciate you bringing this news to me, and would very much like your assistance in locating her."

Daku nodded, clearly relieved this hadn't turned into a physical altercation. "I would be happy to help."

"Great," Jade said. "Let's head down to the kitchen."

Chapter 7

alakai, Daku, Tristan, Reya, Talon, Jade, Raven, Embry, and I gathered in the kitchen. The rest joined the others outside, to catch them up on what had happened.

"Can you tell us more about your visions?" Embry asked Daku.

"It is difficult to describe. When our spirits drift, we connect with other spirits. Unless we come across another who is aware, we really don't even see their physical form."

"Does that mean my sister is aware?"

"That is a question I cannot answer. I am constantly drawn to her, I can see her, but she has yet to respond to me."

Malakai folded his hands on the table and spoke. "In my time, I've only come across a handful of souls who were aware. Only one that I ever had a conversation with—Reya's mother. She had the same capabilities, and so was able to manifest physically and verbally. That is not usually the case."

"Do you think you're drawn to her because she needs help?" Embry asked, his eyebrows knitting as he attempted to understand.

"Possibly."

Though I didn't want to expose my own ability in front of all these people, I felt the need to speak up. "There is another possibility."

All eyes were on me. "What is that, sweetheart?"

"Daku could be drawn to her…because she could be his mate." The young man in question visibly paled, though I noticed this idea didn't shock him. Embry studied him with renewed intensity and interest.

"That makes sense," Jade said. "Mates have an insanely strong connection. I connected to Talon's memories, Reya and Tristan found each other in dreams. Reese also dreamt about Dominic's past, and Samson did the same with Lani. Kate helped Hugh unlock his memories."

"We are still learning about the connection between mates," Reya said. "Unfortunately, it seems we have lost our older generation and have to discover things anew. Reese and Arie had an interesting theory regarding Emerson, though. He's able to not only speak with her telepathically, but can almost read her thoughts—or, at least, her emotions. She thinks, because of Emerson's unique ability, that he's essentially honed his mental muscles and that we all have the possibility of doing the same."

"Elementals are full of untapped potential," Malakai agreed.

"Only our imaginations limit us," I murmured, looking up at Embry. His gaze met mine, and he offered a soft smile.

"My mate is correct. This is an important topic to discuss, and I personally would like to go into great detail at a later time—but forgive me for steering us back to my sister."

"Of course," Reya said instantly. "Forgive us. I can only imagine how you're feeling. Daku, did you have any ideas on how to locate Rika?"

"I was hoping you and Damien would be willing to help. If we could somehow link our powers, we may be able to find her."

Tristan nodded and wrapped his arm around Reya's shoulder. "We will delay our travel plans as long as necessary to assist you with this. Talon, may we make use of one of your homes?"

"Of course," Talon answered.

"We've got extra space where our family was staying," I offered. "Plenty of room for all of you."

"Father? Is it all right if I miss a few more days of school?" Daku asked.

Malakai laughed. "For something this important, I'd say it's warranted."

"It's a plan," Reya said. "Damien and Daku, let's move our luggage and then discuss some ideas. Embry and Valentina, we'd love to have you in on that conversation."

When Reya looked at me, I understood what she implied. It was time to tell Embry the truth about me.

We left Jade's home and said good-bye to the group still leaving that day. Several offered their assistance in the search for Rika, and Embry assured them he would call upon them if needed. Raven left with Tristan and Reya to help with luggage, and I was certain to spend some time with the twins. Though she played it cool about relationships, I knew Raven had a soft spot for children.

Embry and I decided to walk back; under mutual agreement we needed some time to clear our heads. I knew he could tell something was wrong and he reached over and casually linked our hands together, showing me support without pressuring me to talk. As we entered the woods, I let out a sigh, forcing myself to spill. "Here's the thing. I have a certain...ability."

"That's wonderful," he said automatically.

"Not always." When I didn't continue, I could feel Embry's eyes on me, searching my expression. He didn't connect psychically, which I appreciated. Though he couldn't exactly read my thoughts, he could feel my emotions and I needed to get this out in my own time. "I'm able to see possible futures."

"You're a seer?" he asked, a note of surprise in his tone.

"Yes. No. I mean, I don't think it works the same as Reya or Damien. I spoke with them both a little, to see how their ability works. Mine is more like, when I'm looking at something, I can see something else happening in that same spot, or to the person I'm looking at."

"Can you give me an example?"

Daku and Rika came to mind, but I ignored that for now. Instead, I told him the same innocuous examples I'd told Reya earlier. "When I was waitressing, I would approach a table to take an order, and all of a sudden I'd see a different group of people sitting there. Or at my parents' house, it'd be springtime but when I walked into the living room, I'd see all the Christmas decorations out. Things like that."

"And these visions just come to you?"

"Yes. Randomly. They usually come and go within a few seconds. Or they did. Damien helped me to sort of force one."

"That is interesting. Abilities, while relatively the same, manifest differently in each person. Even Damien and Reya, though they are both seers, it doesn't work exactly the same for them. And Damien told me of his sister—he lost her, too—while she also could see the future, what she could do was wildly different from what he could do."

Not only did I find that fascinating, but it also pushed off me admitting what I'd seen earlier. "How did hers work?"

"The way Damien described it, she could literally see the flow of time. If she picked a flower, she would see all the consequences of that action. She could roll a ball into a street and set off a chain of events that either saved lives or hindered them."

What he described boggled my mind. "What a horrible thing to live with."

"What do you mean?"

"You could never really live, could you? Knowing, every time you stepped outside, what every single one of your actions would affect. I wouldn't want that responsibility."

"I didn't think about it that way," Embry conceded. "But you're correct. That would be a heavy burden to bear."

"What happened to her?"

"Damien doesn't know. His story is similar to mine, unfortunately. He turned to the darkness after he lost her."

What an awful way to live. And now, I knew something that could give Embry hope. Was it selfish of me to hold onto that? "Embry, I forced a vision of Daku."

"You did? What of?"

"Well, I saw him...and your sister."

For a moment we walked in silence. The sun had come out and pushed back the cool breeze. When Embry spoke again, his voice remained calm. "You believe they're mates."

"I do."

"What can you tell me about your vision? Was she...was she okay? Did she look happy?"

"They were sitting together. I could see the love between them. She was smiling at him, and then she looked straight at me. Or straight at someone, where I was standing. Her eyes are so much like yours, deep and intense. They seemed happy. But..."

"But what?"

"Daku was older. Much older. A man. This was years from now, at least. Longer, if Daku becomes an Elemental."

Embry took this information in stride. "He is only a boy. This is a lot of pressure to put on him, though I can see how protective he already feels toward her."

"You think I shouldn't tell him?"

He sighed and paused to face me. "I think you should do whatever you feel is right."

"I wasn't going to tell him. The idea that Rika is his mate is already in his mind, but telling him about how long it could be— that could change his decisions too drastically."

"I agree with you. But thank you for telling me. For trusting me, and for giving me hope. You will never know what that means to me."

"We're going to find her. No matter what." Reaching up, I placed my palm along his jaw. His eyes darkened to metal as I stared up at him. Slowly, carefully, he lowered his mouth to mine. Just as slowly I rose on my toes to meet him. We came together to soothe, to comfort. To ignite.

His arms wrapped around my waist and I braced myself against his broad shoulders. The world around us spun and clashed as his soft lips pressed against mine, his tongue teasing along the seam of my mouth.

I opened to him on a sigh. Wrapped my fingers in the tangle of wavy hair falling across his shoulders. He lifted me to my toes, then off them. Not fully realizing what I was doing, I wrapped my legs around his waist and clung to him as fire erupted in my veins.

His hands slipped from my waist, traveled under my shirt to trace along my ribs. When he cupped my breasts, my head fell back with a gasp.

He breathed in the scent of my neck, nipped and teased the sensitive skin there. I'd never been touched like this, kissed like this. The sensations made my head swim, my body ache. I wasn't thinking anymore. Couldn't think anything except: more.

With a groan that sounded an awful lot like a growl, Embry's wandering hands returned to my waist and held me tight. He lifted his head and his beautiful eyes glittered down at me.

Still riding a strange high, I blinked up at him in confusion. "Why did you stop?"

"Believe me, I do not wish to. But we are in the woods. Anyone could come upon us, and I'm afraid I would not even notice. You are an innocent, and I would like to take my time, show you true pleasure. Perhaps in a bed, instead of against a tree."

A crazy part of my brain wanted to fight him, make him finish what he'd started. Then, the logical part finally got some air and forced me to see his reasoning. "You're right. I hate it, but you're right. Okay. Put me down. But don't let go, because I don't think my legs will work."

He chuckled and eased me to the ground. Putting my weight on unsteady feet, I held onto him until I felt positive I wouldn't just crumble. "Ready?"

"I think so," I replied. "Just tell me you're as shaky as I am."

"Valentina, you have affected every fiber of my being. You make me weak, and yet stronger than I've ever felt. You have filled my heart with light and goodness where I thought only darkness could exist. For that alone, I would love you. Yet I find myself constantly surprised by you. You are the most compassionate, loving, amazing person I've ever met. I know we've only just met, and you may not feel the same way yet, but I love you. And I know that my love for you will only grow stronger with time."

He floored me with his words. My mouth opened to respond but snapped shut again. We'd only met days ago. How could I truly know my feelings so quickly?

"Do not think you have to respond. I just wanted to tell you how I feel. I am still willing to take our relationship as slowly as you need." When I couldn't think of anything else to say, I nodded. He placed a sweet, chaste kiss against my lips before stepping away. The loss of his heat left me shivering, but the strong, hot hand he wrapped around mine steadied me again. "Are you ready?"

"Yes. We should get back."

I had a lot of things to think about.

Chapter 8

A smaller group gathered in the living room where Tristan and Reya would stay for however long they needed. Malakai, Daku, Tristan, Reya, Damien, Embry, and Valentina were there to discuss a way to find Rika and bring her home.

Embry had a difficult time believing his sister could actually be out there somewhere. Alone, but alive. He hadn't felt hope like this for a very long time. Valentina had brought the first light into his life after so many years of darkness; having his sister back would make him feel truly whole again.

Daku, though only fourteen, had been through *koradji* training and was seen as a man by his people. Malakai was the acknowledged leader of the *koradji*, and Daku inherited all the respect of a *koradji* who received the visions and as the next in line to lead.

"We can perform a ritual tonight in order to determine Rika's location," Daku suggested.

Damien looked first to Reya and then to Valentina. "Would you both be willing to link powers? I believe it is our best chance of locating her."

"Yes, I'm willing," Reya said.

Valentina took a deep breath. Embry nearly burst with pride at her strength. "As am I."

"Once you three combine your talents, Reya can connect with Daku and myself," Malakai said. "We can spirit travel together."

"What can I do?" Embry asked.

Damien was the one to answer. "You have the strongest connection to her. You should be in the protected circle with us. Connect with your mate and focus everything you have on finding your sister."

Tristan didn't seem comfortable with being left out. Malakai addressed him before he could voice his complaint. "Tristan, along with Grey and Jericho, will form a protective ring. Spirit traveling is a dangerous business. Our bodies will be vulnerable while our souls drift."

"Three circles of three," Reya murmured. "There is power in nine."

"Then we are agreed?" Malakai asked. When no one protested, he gave a determined nod. "Midnight it is."

∞ ∞ ∞

EMBRY STAYED WITH VALENTINA THROUGH the rest of the evening. Raven pouted at dinner about being left out. "Are you sure there's nothing I can do?"

"I'm sorry, you know I wish you could be there. But Reya says there's power in nine."

"There's more power in ten."

"You know that's not how magic works."

"Okay, okay. But you come straight home, you hear me?" Raven pointed her finger between Embry and Valentina.

"I will ensure her safety," Embry promised, "and bring her straight home."

"Okay. I guess that's good enough."

As midnight approached, Embry could see the nerves on Valentina's face. She'd barely told anyone of her powers before this, and now she was attempting a powerful and potentially dangerous spell. Embry took her hand between his and waited for her to meet his gaze. "You can do this, sweetheart. You are stronger and more powerful than you know."

"And if it doesn't work?"

"Then we try something else."

She nodded and let out a deep breath as the others joined them outside. They had chosen a location far enough away from the sleeping babies and other innocents—just in case.

Grey and Jericho were waiting for them. Each greeted Embry in turn and murmured encouragement. He took whatever they had to offer.

Together they watched as Malakai, Daku, and Damien set the protection circle. Embry had never been as talented with spells, but he watched with rapt fascination. He stepped into the inner circle when directed, followed by Valentina and the other seers. Finally, Tristan, Grey, and Jericho closed ranks.

Daku sat cross-legged in the center, with Malakai and Embry following suit. The two *koradji* had painted symbols upon their faces, a way of calling to their ancestors for assistance. As they began chanting in their native tongue, Embry closed his eyes and brought up his memories of Rika.

He felt Valentina's presence, light as a feather. He opened himself completely to her. Shared his memories even as he remembered them. The fun times. The tragic ones.

Around him, Damien, Reya, and Valentina linked hands and concentrated. A swirl of wind, contained within their circle, whipped hair and sought answers.

Our ancestors are gauging our intentions. Embry didn't know for certain whose voice that was or how it got into his mind, but he didn't question. He simply accepted.

Power reverberated within the circle. Embry felt himself slipping into his past. His sister running ahead of him, her laughter floating back on the wind. They were barefoot, the earth responding to every footfall. It was a time before the darkness. They were happy. Carefree.

The earth shook with a great boom. Embry fell back with a gasp, the circle broken. He opened his eyes and sought out Valentina first; she'd fallen but assured him she was fine. The rest of the group picked themselves off the ground in varying degrees of disappointment and frustration.

None more so than Daku. He kicked at the broken circle. "It didn't work." He cringed with pain, but took a few steps away and back again, calming himself. "I'm afraid we're going to need more help."

Malakai seemed to be the only one who understood. "We need to gather the *koradji*."

"It's our best chance," Daku agreed.

"Gather the *koradji*? Where?"

"Australia." Daku looked to Damien. "Did you see anything?"

The seers glanced between each other. "Only one thing was clear; she is not in this world."

Tristan spoke up. "The otherworld?"

"We believe so," Reya answered. "Whether she is in Murias or not was unclear."

Silence settled upon the group. Tristan rubbed his chin thoughtfully. "How quickly can you gather the *koradji*?"

"We would need a few days, at least."

"I have an idea where we can kill two birds with one stone."

"What do you mean?" Reya asked.

"We can go to Australia, Malakai can gather the *koradji*, and we will prepare for another ritual—on Samhain."

"You want to be a distraction for the Murias group?" Embry asked, picking up Tristan's train of thought easily.

"Yes."

They all stared at each other in shock. It just might work. Malakai nodded enthusiastically. "Let's do it."

"Samhain is not quite two weeks away. Is that enough time?" Reya asked.

"It should be. We need to return home, prepare."

Valentina squeezed Embry's hand. She spoke, knowing they would be on the same page. "We will join you."

Daku nodded. "That would be appreciated. You won't have to come right away—just a few days before. Of course, for us, it will be springtime."

"Beltane," Reya said. "Still a powerful time. It will also be, oh, about nine o'clock in the morning in Ayers Rock when it's midnight in Ireland."

"It's also a new moon," Tristan said. "We'll be hitting them at their weakest. Spring, where new life is beginning. Daytime, and a new moon."

"He has a good point," Daku said. "It's decided, then."

"Looks like we're going home," Reya said, wrapping her arm around Tristan's waist.

"I'll have the plane ready first thing in the morning," Tristan promised Malakai. "Embry, Valentina, when you're ready, I will make sure one of our planes is available."

Flying to Australia in a private jet? Sounds too good to be true.

Embry smiled at his mate even as he answered. "That sounds amazing, thank you."

Chapter 9

Standing in the doorway with Embry by my side, I hesitated before knocking. There were going to be a lot of people in there. This felt almost more terrifying than introducing Embry to my own family.

The group traveling to Ireland—including Samson and Lani—had left yesterday morning. Before they'd left, I'd asked Jade to sketch out a picture like she'd done for Daku. I described the woman in my vision with Frances, deciding to tell him of the potential and giving him the picture as hope.

We could all use more hope.

And since we were staying a couple more weeks, I knew we couldn't get out of dinner with the Callaghans.

"Are you all right?" Embry asked, his palm resting at the small of my back.

"Yes," I squeaked out. Trying again, I said, "Yes. It's just that there are a lot of people in there."

"I will remain by your side," Embry promised.

Making the mistake of looking up at him, I instantly got sucked into his deep gaze. Though I had no intention of moving, I seemed to drift closer to him without effort. We became so wrapped in the intense moment that I didn't hear the shuffle of feet on the other side of the door. It popped open and I'd been caught in a nearly compromising position.

"Valentina!" Pearl said by way of greeting. Winking at Embry, she added, "Hey there, hot stuff."

"Good evening," Embry replied smoothly while I still worked to clear the haze of our private moment.

"Come on in." Pearl punctuated this by grabbing each of our wrists and dragging us inside. "Look who's here!"

We entered the living room to find most of Jade's family staring back at us. Madeline, Amber, and Emma were in the kitchen, finishing the meal. Some of the kids were in the backyard with Rick, Emma's fiancé, and Micah, Pearl's husband. They were joined by Grey, another former shadowman who had found out he had distant relations to Micah.

Which still left us with plenty of pairs of eyes watching us.

Pearl continued to drag us inside until we found ourselves wedged in the middle of the couch between Jack, Amber's husband, and Isaac, Jade's dad.

A couple of the kids climbed over us, one of the younger ones—Sandy—snuggling in Embry's lap. Pearl sat on the coffee table, facing us. I had a sudden image of bright lights and stale coffee.

"So, I hear you two are dating," Pearl began. "That's so great. Tell me all about it."

"Pearl, leave them alone," Jade said in an attempt to come to my rescue, but it was useless.

Pearl waved a dismissive hand in her sister's direction before continuing, "Have you thought about getting married yet? We've become pretty good at wedding planning. How about kids? How many do you each want?"

This is like the Spanish Inquisition, I groaned.

I lived through the Spanish Inquisition, he sent back. *This is worse.*

His unexpected joke forced a bubble of laughter to escape from my lips. Pearl's eyes narrowed, not understanding where my sudden humor had come from.

An older man with kind eyes approached Pearl from behind, laying his hands on her shoulders. "Come now, Pearl. Leave these children be. They'll figure things out in their own time."

"But, Grandpa..." Pearl began to protest, but Mr. Stryder shook his head.

"She's been like this since she was a child. Did I ever tell you kids about the man on the beach with the genie?"

"I don't think I've heard that," I said hesitantly.

"A man finds a lamp on a beach. A genie pops out and says he can have one wish, anything he wants. So, the man asks for a freeway to Hawaii. The genie says no, it's not possible. Ask for something else, anything else. The man says, all right, I want to truly understand women. What they want, the way they think. The genie ponders that for a while and says, 'did you want that freeway two lanes or four?'"

I chuckled with the rest of the room. Pearl pouted, and when I saw her about to take the opening to ask more questions, I wiggled my way off the couch and grabbed Embry's hand. "How about some fresh air?"

Sandy looked up at him with puppy-dog eyes. "Me too?"

"Sure, little one," Embry agreed, standing easily with her in his arms.

He followed me to the sliding door off the dining room where I took a grateful gulp of the crisp air. Grey turned and greeted us while Sandy pointed at the swing-set the other kids played on.

"Swing?" she asked Embry.

He had a difficult time resisting her charms. While he took Sandy over to the swings, I swiped the lemonade from Rick's hands.

"They are a lot to take at once," I complained aloud.

"Tell me about it," Grey sympathized. "I've already been set up with four different women. Four. I've only been here a week."

Rick laughed good-naturedly. "Did you know Pearl set me up with Jade first?"

"No!" I nearly choked. "How did I not know that?"

"Because we were never anything more than friends. I was head over heels for Emma the moment I laid eyes on her—even though she was still married."

Micah shrugged affectionately. "That's my wife. She means well."

I did feel slightly bad for Grey. Little did Pearl know that it wouldn't matter how many times she set him up—there would be only one woman out there for him. But, since Jade's family wasn't exactly up to speed on Elementals, he would have to suffer through.

Though I tried to keep my eyes off him, they continuously traveled back to Embry. He found such joy in the little things—like now, pushing Sandy on the swing as she screamed to go higher. It was an appealing trait, and one that I knew he'd more than earned.

His eyes lifted to mine, his smile lighting a spark in the deep gray. My heart stuttered and stopped before kicking into high gear. I experienced one of those deer-in-headlights moments, rooted to the spot.

Suddenly, another scene transposed itself on top of this one—Embry, with our own child. Me, holding an identical one in my arms. His laughter winging out into the night, as if the wind decided to share his joy with the world.

"Dinner's ready!" Jade called out from the house, shattering the illusion.

I took a step back and shook my head as the kids ran inside, followed more sedately by the other three men. Embry arrived at my side just moments later, looking concerned.

"What is it?" he asked gently.

"N—nothing," I lied.

Valentina, he said softly, his husky voice wrapping around my insides. *One should not lie to their mate.*

We'll talk about it later, I promised before escaping inside.

∞ ∞ ∞

AS EMBRY DROVE ME HOME, I remained quiet as I had all through dinner. He waited patiently for me to spill, but the image of Embry and our future children had shaken me to my core.

"What is it, Valentina? You have been quiet all night."

"I--I'm not sure I can speak about it."

"Did I do something wrong?"

"Oh, no, of course not. It's just—"

Before I could finish, the headlights washed over a street corner not far from the cabin. A woman lay along the sidewalk, her black hair hiding her face, dark smudges of blood soaking into the concrete. A scream welled up through my chest, startling Embry into slamming on the brakes.

Without thought I pushed open the door and ran to the corner, only to find the image gone. I sank to my knees as huge, uncontrollable sobs racked my chest. I felt a gentle hand on my back, and though he attempted calm I could hear the underlying panic in Embry's voice.

"Valentina, what's wrong sweetheart? Are you all right? Talk to me, please."

Turning into his chest, I let the unexpected tears run their course. When I could breathe again, I pulled away, embarrassed. "Raven."

"What about her?" he asked, clearly concerned about my mental stability.

"She...she was right here," I said with a hitch in my voice, pointing a shaking finger toward the sidewalk. "She was bleeding."

Finally understanding, Embry pulled me back into his arms, holding my head against his chest. "Oh, sweetheart, it's all right. She's not here. She's okay."

"But she won't be," I said, my words barely audible. "There was a bike next to her. She must have been riding, and a car..."

"Shh, it's all right. Now that we know, we won't let her out of our sight."

"We need to find her. Now." Determination set on my face, I stood and marched back to the car. "I'll handcuff her to my side if need be."

Embry opened my door and eased me into the seat. As he slid behind the driver's side, I pulled out my phone to call Raven, but after several rings, I got her voicemail. "Call me back, ASAP."

Clasping his warm hand over mine, Embry turned us around and headed back toward the Callaghans'. Though he murmured reassurances, I felt a hot knot of foreboding settle low in my stomach. I tried Jade's phone next, but she didn't answer either.

"If she's on her way home, we'll see her," Embry soothed. "But I'm sure she'll still be at Madeline's. She'll be okay."

I wanted to believe it—but everything inside told me otherwise.

As we pulled onto the Callaghans' street, Jade's number popped up on my phone. "Jade! Where's Raven?"

"She left a few minutes ago," Jade answered. "What's wrong?"

Hot tears leaked down my cheeks as dread took control. I couldn't get the words out. Embry pulled over, taking the phone gently from my hand. "Have Talon meet me at the corner of Fourth and Main. We're outside. Please take Valentina by car."

And with that, he was gone. Jade ran from the house seconds later, taking over the driver's side. "What's going on?"

"Raven...she..." My hysterics were too much for Jade, so she lay a calming hand against my forearm as she put the car in gear. I felt a strange, warm tingling, and the pressure on my chest lessened. Sucking in a full breath, I tried again. "I had a vision of Raven bleeding in the street. We need to get there, now."

To Jade's credit, she didn't even question my ability or what I saw. She merely stepped on the gas while I attempted to keep it together.

Valentina. His voice felt like a breath of fresh air, but I could also hear the underlying tension. *I've found her. She's fading fast, sweetheart. But I can save her. Do you wish me to do this?*

Yes. The tears returned, silently streaking down my cheeks. *Please, save her.*

Jade's hand clasped mine, as Talon must have updated her. "She's going to be fine. Talon and Embry will do whatever they have to."

Jade turned off, avoiding the corner where Raven had been found, broken and bleeding. She headed straight for our cabin, where Embry must have thought to bring Raven. After we parked, Jade came around to help me out of the car. She wrapped an arm around my back and guided me into the house. All our surroundings blurred as I put one foot in front of the other, forcing myself forward even as I wanted to collapse.

We stepped into Raven's room to find her lying with her eyes closed, her body still as death.

Chapter 10

Embry rushed over as soon as I stepped into Raven's room, shielding me from view. "No, I want to see her. Is she—is she going to be all right?"

"We've done everything we can, sweetheart," Embry said gently. "She's strong, she's a fighter. She'll get through this."

"The fever has already set in," Talon murmured from her bedside. "Her pulse has returned, slow but steady."

Even though Embry wanted me to stay away, I trudged forward to Raven's side. I wouldn't leave my best friend now, no matter what condition I found her in. Sinking to my knees, I grasped her hand and studied her through blurry eyes. There was blood everywhere. So much blood.

Jade appeared next to me with a bowl of warm, soapy water and a washcloth. "We'll get her cleaned up. She's going to be fine, Valentina."

"We need to call Samson. He'll want to be here."

"I already have," Talon said. "He and Lani are returning as quickly as they are able."

"Who did this?" Silence met my whispered question. I could tell there was something they weren't telling me. Looking up at Embry, I said, "Tell me. What is it?"

"It was a hit and run," Embry finally admitted. "We believe we saw the vehicle driving away when we arrived. Grey and Jericho are out searching for it now."

I hadn't realized my hands shook until Embry laid his over mine and Raven's. His reassuring presence gave me strength I didn't possess. I knew it had been difficult for Embry to let the person who did this get away, but Raven's health was more important. To both of us.

I'd always considered her my family. And now, Embry did too.

I sat with Raven late into the night. Only when my eyes began to droop did Embry carry me to my room. He left me in privacy to change, but I headed straight back to Raven's side. Curling up on the bed beside her, I felt the tears I'd been fighting begin to fall.

Embry didn't try to speak, he just let me feel. He remained by my side, even after I fell into a fitful sleep. When I woke, his gray eyes were the first thing I saw.

"She's warm," Embry said. "That means she's undergoing the change."

"Thank you," I whispered, turning back to my best friend. I couldn't leave her side. Not until her eyes opened again.

Three days went by; the longest three days of my life. Though Embry tried, he couldn't get me to move from Raven's side. I ate when he begged me and slept in patches. Finally, on the third night, Raven let out a moan as her eyes fluttered open.

"Raven!" Attacking her with a hug, I eased back when she made a distressed noise. "What? What's wrong?"

"Don't take this the wrong way, but you stink. When's the last time you showered?"

I laughed, tears of joy streaking down my cheeks. We hugged again before she began to ask the serious questions.

Embry told her in his calmest voice what had happened. I listened, my heart breaking all over again, more tears escaping as he got to the part I hadn't been there for. When he'd found Raven on the sidewalk, unconscious and near death.

"Wow," Raven finally said. "I—I don't really know what to say."

Samson and Lani were in the room, listening to the story for the second time. Samson hugged his sister, his own emotions getting the better of him. "I'm so glad you're all right. Don't ever scare me again, you hear me?"

"I'll do my best."

I finally stood and wiped my face. Embry opened his mouth to speak, but I stopped him. *Just give me a minute.*

Escaping into my room, I let out a breath it felt like I'd been holding since the night Raven had been struck. All the tension had eased from my limbs the moment her eyes had finally opened again.

Embry had been so amazing over the last few days. Not only saving Raven's life but taking care of me the way he had. Giving me the space I needed even while making sure my basic needs were taken care of. The way he'd watched over both me and Raven.

I grabbed fresh clothes and took a shower, realizing just how gross I'd actually gotten. The fact that Embry had stayed so close to me without complaining was a miracle in and of itself.

When I stepped out, Raven was on her feet. She smiled at me, looking no worse for the wear. "We're going hunting."

"You're ready for that?"

"We'll take it easy," Lani promised. "But she needs to feed. It will be the fastest way to regain her strength."

I hugged Raven. "I love you."

"I love you, too. I'll be back soon."

"You better."

Squeezing her hands, I stepped back into my room to finish getting dressed. So much had become clear to me. I now knew exactly what I wanted. No hesitations.

I felt more than heard Embry step into the room. We were alone in the house. Perfect.

Turning, I launched myself at him before he could even speak. My mouth closed over his with a frenzy. Though surprised by the move, Embry quickly caught up. His hands wrapped around my waist then slid up into my hair. He took control of the kiss, adjusting my head to a new, deeper angle.

My hands smoothed over his chest, slid to his hemline. Lifted his shirt up, forcing the kiss to break for a moment. I sucked in a breath first from his kiss, and then from seeing his bare skin. Before he could take control again, I placed my fingertips against his muscles, traced each intriguing line as I'd wanted to do from the moment we met in the woods.

I placed my lips against his rapidly beating heart, and then stepped back to lift my own shirt over my head. When I dropped it to the floor, I had the pleasure of watching Embry's eyes turn to liquid silver.

"Valentina, are you certain?"

"I've never been more certain about anything in my life."

He needed no more convincing. His mouth captured mine as his hands memorized every inch of my skin. More clothes fell to the floor until we were finally able to press against each other, skin to skin. He lifted me from my feet and lay me back on the bed with infinite tenderness. His mouth explored where his hands had already touched, and I arched back as waves of pleasure washed over me.

With one hand he gripped my wrists over my head and looked deep into my eyes. Watched the expressions flit over my face as he joined us so gently together. When we were fully one, he asked, "Are you all right?"

There had been a little bit of pain, but so much more pleasure. Nodding, I pressed my lips to his. "More than all right."

He moved then, slow and easy. It built a fire low in my stomach. He continued to fan the flames until the conflagration took over, shot along every vein and out of my fingers and toes. I gasped and shuddered and gripped his hands tightly, afraid if I let go, I would spiral away from the earth and into the stars.

Embry rested his head under my chin, his breath gradually slowing along with our hearts. I felt limp, deliciously sore, and utterly satisfied.

He lifted his head, gently kissed my swollen lips. Framing his face with my hands, I spoke from the heart. "I love you, Embry Jain."

"As I do you, Valentina Stone."

Chapter 11

As the plane began its descent, I reached over and grasped Raven's hand. This would be the first time either of us had stepped foot outside the States. Hell, before Jade and Talon's wedding, we hadn't been outside New Mexico.

Wisconsin had been vastly different from our home, but the wide length of sand that greeted us in Australia felt right.

Embry sat beside me, claiming my other hand. Now that we'd taken the next step in our relationship, I had a difficult time keeping my hands off him. That proved interesting when we'd been on a plane with my family for the last eighteen hours or so.

Are you nervous?

A little. Are you?

We can face anything together, Embry answered, sending a fresh wave of heat through me.

Raven squeezed my hand and smirked; her newfound supernatural abilities could be so annoying.

Gary set us down in Ayers Rock Airport, in the town of Yulara, the closest inhabitation to the sacred site. Malakai and his family lived on the land as his family had for generations, but he practiced law in Yulara.

We exited the plane and I took a deep breath of the hot, dry air. The summer season had just begun, and it felt like home. Tristan and Reya met us with two SUVs, and we drove first to the resort we'd be staying in.

"Malakai has asked us to meet with them in two hours," Reya told us after we checked in. "I'm sure you'd all like to wash up or rest before then. Tristan and I will be back to pick you up at six-thirty."

Embry carried our luggage to our suite overlooking the sand dunes. I'd never stayed in any place so nice in my life.

"Would you like to rest?" Embry asked.

"No," I said, shaking my head with a smirk. "First, I want a shower. And you're joining me."

FEELING VERY RELAXED, WE HEADED down to wait for the rest of our group in the lobby. Tristan and Reya arrived as promised, and we drove together to meet with Malakai. We would come back to our rooms later that night, and then make our way up the red mountain before sunrise tomorrow.

Embry and I rode with Reya and Raven, while Tristan took Samson and Lani. Reya told us we would have dinner with Malakai's family. About three hundred Pitjantjatjara Anangu still inhabited the area around Ayers Rock—Malakai's family included.

We drove through the National Park and down dirt roads until we came upon the Anangu's home. Squat buildings grouped together dotted the landscape and I could see men, women, and children working and playing outside.

Reya pulled in behind Tristan and I saw Malakai exit his home with his wife, children, and Reya's twins close behind. Damien, who had been speaking with a group of men a few homes away, came over as well.

"Palya," Malakai greeted us with open arms. "Welcome. How was your journey?"

"Wonderful, thank you," I said, hugging him.

"We have prepared a feast for you tonight," Malakai said after he'd embraced each of us. "We will eat and dance in preparation of our ceremony. It will notify our ancestors of our intent to ask for help."

With that, he led us to a clear area with a beautiful view of Ayers Rock—known locally as Uluru. It shone a bright red in the setting sun, and for a moment I stood and stared with Embry by my side.

"Come, sit. I hope you're hungry," Malakai said, gesturing for us to join those already in attendance.

Women wore simple cotton dresses and carried wooden bowls filled with food. A bonfire had been lit in the center, doubling as light and a way to cook. The distinct notes of a didgeridoo filled the air as I settled on the ground between Raven and Embry, gratefully taking samples of offered dishes. There was a variety of smoked and roasted meats, along with a collection of fruits, vegetables, and roots I didn't recognize.

We ate our fill as many of the tribe came over to speak to us. Not all spoke English, so Daku and his sister, Kalinda, joined our group to translate. Another woman approached with a bowl of...ants. Their tiny bodies looked like the familiar black ant, but their abdomens bubbled out in an amber-colored sphere.

"What are these?" I asked.

"Honey ants," Daku replied, taking one and holding it up.

"Ants?"

"They are found using a wana—a digging stick. Hold the body and pop the abdomen into your mouth," Daku instructed, watching with amusement at our hesitation. "They're sweet, I promise."

Looking to Raven, I shrugged and picked one up. "I'm game if you are."

"Count of three?" she asked. "One, two, three..."

We both popped the abdomens into our mouths, and I found myself shocked at the taste. "It *is* sweet."

"That's why they're called honey ants," Daku said with a laugh.

I felt Embry chuckle beside me, so I elbowed him in the ribs even knowing it wouldn't have any effect on him. We thanked the woman before she moved on with her delicacy. I spotted a bowl with small, green plums called kakadu, and I made sure to grab a few before they passed on. "Everything is wonderful, Daku."

"I'm glad you're enjoying it. The dancing will begin soon—actually, I better go join the others. The visiting shaman and I will be performing to open communication with the spirits."

"Sounds wonderful. Can't wait to see it," Raven said.

He gave us his signature little-boy smile before rising easily off the ground and loping to the opposite side of the campfire.

"Will you also go through shaman training?" I asked Kalinda. She'd been quiet while her brother had been here, but I knew from watching her and Kai at the wedding that she was anything but shy.

She nodded. "I have been lucidly dreaming as long as I can remember, and it is tradition in our family to go through the training."

"From what I understand, there aren't very many women who achieve such status."

"That is true." Her gaze shifted to the koradji preparing for the dance. "But one with the gift is not ignored."

"When will your training begin?"

"After the summer season, when I turn thirteen."

"So young," I murmured, seeing wisdom beyond her years in her curious gaze.

Embry squeezed my hand as silence settled over the crowd gathered. After a few moments, drums joined the lonely notes of the didgeridoo. Daku had been painted for the dance, as had the rest of the shaman with him. Their feet pounded the ground as their arms rotated in one large circle. A chant rose up from the crowd in the Pitjantjatjara language. Beautiful and haunting.

Embry's arm wrapped around my back, his fingers secure around my waist. I leaned into him as the dance wore on, appreciating his warmth as the night temperatures began to drop.

The festivities lasted well into the night. At some point I fell asleep against Embry, waking briefly as we loaded into the car, and again as he carried me into our room. He stripped me down, not bothering with pajamas, before tucking me under the sheets. When he joined me, his hot skin keeping me toasty warm, I snuggled in and allowed my dreams to overtake me.

I WOKE IN A PANIC, my breath coming out in sobs. Embry held me tight, whispering soothing nonsense into my ear.

"It was just a dream, sweetheart. Just a dream."

How could I tell him it wasn't? The truth was, I couldn't. The only thing I knew was that I needed comfort. I needed a distraction. I needed Embry.

My mouth found his in desperation. I pressed myself against him, wanting—needing—to feel him against me. In a move that surprised us both, I rolled him to his back and straddled him. Took him inside me without breaking for a breath. There was a frenzy of need and lust raging to be let loose.

I didn't hold back. Neither did he. We rose together and just as quickly fell together. But it didn't stop there. Embry gripped my hips, forced me over the edge again. I spiraled happily, panting for breath. He held me close, pressed my head against his chest so I could hear his rapidly beating heart. We were still connected in the most intimate way, and I never wanted to part.

"I'm sorry," I breathed against him.

"Believe me, Valentina," he replied with amusement. "You have nothing to apologize for."

Propping my head up so I could see his expression, I said, "But I basically just attacked you."

"I am not complaining." He brushed my hair back, his mirth fading. "What was your dream about? You were obviously upset by it."

"I—I think I connected to your memories," I admitted. "It was the day you lost Rika."

"Oh, sweetheart," he said, pulling me close again. "I'm so sorry you had to live through that."

"In a strange way, I'm glad I did. It helps me understand you better, anyway."

"You are the strongest woman I've ever met," he murmured in my ear. "I'm so lucky to have you in my life. I love you, Valentina Stone."

I looked up again, smiled softly. "I love you, too."

Chapter 12

Embry and I spent the day playing tourist with Raven, Samson, and Lani. Tristan, Reya, the twins, and Damien joined us for lunch, where we sat with a stunning view of Uluru.

As the sun began its descent, we headed back to the National Park. Malakai's tribe had closed the area to tourists, citing sacred reasons. Malakai met us in the parking area as we all climbed out of the vehicles.

"Welcome to Uluru," Malakai greeted us, then led the way. "Please, follow me. This is a sacred place for our people. Would you like to hear the tale of our people?"

"Love to," most of us answered aloud, while the rest nodded their heads.

"In the beginning, there was nothing. The land was flat, and free from plants and animals. Ten of our ancestors, our spirit people, walked the earth and created the hills and seas, the trees and animals. They helped form our tribes and showed us how to live.

"When they were no longer needed, our spirit people began to disappear from our view, but they were not gone. They became the earth and sky, fire and rain. They live on in sacred places, watching the world from beyond.

"This has become known as our 'dreamtime.' As each new generation comes into adulthood, they are taught to commune with our ancestors and learn from them. In this, the past, present, and future all exist simultaneously."

Malakai led us down the deserted Mala path to the base of the trail leading up the mountain. I spotted signs asking visitors not to climb, but I also knew those didn't stop the determined.

"Climbing Uluru can be dangerous, and it is sacred to my people. We welcome outsiders to learn of our history and culture, but not all are respectful of the land. We only climb on rare occasions. Please step carefully."

Embry kept hold of my hand, and we walked side by side. A railing had been installed to assist those making the trek to the top. Our group remained unusually quiet as we walked, the only sounds coming from the wind and few animals scurrying about before night struck.

When we reached the top, the mountain flattened like a plateau. It offered gorgeous views of the surrounding lands as the brilliant colors of sunset shot across the sky.

It's beautiful, I sent to Embry, not wanting to interrupt the serenity of the silence.

As are you, Embry replied, sending a delicious wave of heat through my system.

We continued to follow Malakai, to where a group of straight-faced men and women waited. They wore little clothing, and it took me a moment to recognize the smiling faces from the night before. These were shaman; the time for celebration had ended, and the stoic group before me waited to perform their duties.

Daku stood center, and he suddenly looked older than his fourteen years. I couldn't imagine doing what he did at his age; when Raven and I had been teens, we'd been whining to our parents about going to concerts. But here he stood, as respected as his father before him, about to undergo a dangerous ceremony to find a missing woman.

"Please, wait here while we make final preparations for the ritual," Malakai said. "This will take most of the night." When we nodded, he turned and clasped arms with his brother, Braithe. Both men were considered leaders of an elite group of koradji.

We watched as they prepared the space and set protections. They chanted in their language and performed similar dances to the night before, this time without the same mirth.

Finally, Malakai and his brother came together again. They lifted wooden bowls that had already been prepared with red paint made from ground ochre, along with white paint created from a clay called kaolin. The brothers used their fingers to paint designs on the faces of the koradji, in addition to any exposed skin.

When this was done, Malakai approached our group. "These symbols help us to communicate with our ancestors. I will apply it to your faces also, so that they recognize you as friend."

We all nodded, and I watched as he began with Embry. The simple yet beautiful designs transformed him from gentle mate to fierce warrior. I went next, and I could only imagine what the paint did for me.

"Gather around," Malakai said when he finished. "The sun rises."

We stood in a circle as the sun appeared, heavy and bright. The men and few women who had undergone shaman training sat in a circle with Daku in the center. He had become the integral piece of this ceremony, given his connection to Rika.

Malakai and his brother began chanting in their native language, joined by the impressive group surrounding Daku. He'd explained the ritual the night before; they would first create a safe space, and then open themselves to the spirits. Daku would ask his favor, and he—perhaps along with the rest of the shaman—would go into a trance if the spirits complied.

All of the koradji had their eyes closed, though their lips continued to move. A breeze swept through our group, tugging at my hair with increasing pressure. Tristan, Reya, Damien, Lani,

Samson, Raven, Embry, and I took the brunt of the force, as it seemed the inner circle remained untouched. The wind seemed to pass straight through me, and I shivered from the contact.

All at once, the air stilled. I realized it hadn't been wind at all—it had been the spirit of their ancestors, much like the circle we'd attempted in Wisconsin.

Whatever test they'd performed, it seemed we passed, for Malakai's eyes popped open, though the blank stare told me he had no control over his voice or limbs. When he spoke, his voice sounded echoey, hollow. Eerie. It surrounded us, coming from everywhere and nowhere at once. "Who has called this gathering?"

"I have," Daku replied. Only then did I realize they spoke in their native tongue—yet I understood perfectly. I wondered if it was the spirits' or Samson's doing.

"What do you ask of us?"

"I seek Rika Jain. She is in trouble and needs our help. Please, great spirits. Help us find her."

The temperature dropped then spiked; the wind returned. I felt Embry's shock, but my vocal cords had been frozen. So had my body. I couldn't move, couldn't speak. The spirits held us in place.

"Do you truly understand what you ask?"

"I do. I am prepared."

"Very well. Request granted."

The earth shook, rumbled. Had I not still been frozen in place, I would have been on my ass. A strange light began to emanate from Daku, rivaling the sun above. No one moved. No one *could* move. We all stared as he rose above the ground, still in his cross-legged position. Eyes closed. Only Malakai's eyes remained open, but the milky appearance told me he couldn't truly see.

I could tell the members of our group wanted to do something, anything. But none of us could move.

With a great crack, the earth split open before us. My jaw wanted to drop open as I watched Daku simply slip through. With an ear-splitting collision, the earth slammed closed again. The spell broke and we all flew back.

Landing with a huff, I groaned and struggled to stand. The circle of koradji had also been knocked back, and they were all blinking the world back into focus. Malakai stood first, staring at the spot his son had just been.

Embry came to my side in an instant, checking me over for injuries. When I assured him that I would be fine, he turned to Malakai. "What happened? Where did he go?"

For the first time, I saw the older man falter. "I—I don't know."

The other shaman seemed baffled, as well. And a little freaked out. Not that I could blame them—the earth had just swallowed Daku whole.

"He's all right," Damien spoke up. "I don't know where he is, I can't see that. But I can see that he will return to us in time."

We all exchanged concerned glances. My gaze sought out Malakai, watched as grief hardened into determination. A vision superimposed itself on the scene—I saw him here, at the top of Ayers Rock, alone. The sunset blared behind him as he waited for his son to return.

A second vision, and then a third. The same, yet different. They kept coming, as if I watched a flipbook unfold. Malakai, returning each day, awaiting the reappearance of his only son. Heat and cold, rain and stars. Without fail, Malakai sought out answers every single day.

I'd never been hit with so many visions at once. I couldn't take it anymore—with a cry of pain, I collapsed back to the hard ground.

Chapter 13

Even when I became aware, my body and mind felt too heavy to move. I drifted through the dark aimlessly until I finally heard a sound. "Valentina." That voice—the only sound that could cut through the darkness and reach me—it was my guiding light. My anchor in a sea of darkness. "Valentina, come back to me."

Struggling to do just that, I managed to lift my lashes for the briefest moment. It all seemed too bright. "That's it, sweetheart. Open your eyes."

Groaning with pain, I forced my lids open halfway. Embry's beloved face filled my vision, and I felt my lips tip up at the corners. "God, you're sexy."

He chuckled, then spoke into my mind. *I'm glad you think so, but I should tell you, we're surrounded by people.*

Oh. Oops. What did I care? Embry held me in his arms. That's all that truly mattered. From the lack of a bruise on my head,

I imagined he'd caught me before I completely hit the ground. That much was good, anyway.

"Help me up," I said aloud, wanting to know what had happened during my blackout. Embry complied, but kept a good grip around my waist. "What happened?"

"You looked like you had a vision," Reya said gently. She'd been close—I'm sure she'd examined me while I'd been out. "And then you fainted. Can you tell us what you saw?"

Looking over at Malakai, I felt my heart sink. How to tell him? "I didn't see Daku. All I know is that it will be a long time before he returns. Possibly...years."

I saw how hard this hit him. He did his best to remain strong in front of his fellow koradji, but I knew something more that could help him.

"Malakai, when we were in Wisconsin, I had a vision of Daku. It was years from now; he was no longer a boy but a man. He was with Rika." Here I looked at Embry, stroked along his jaw. "I believe they're mates. I don't know where he is, but I believe it's the only way he's going to find her. One day, they'll both return. Together. And they're going to be happy."

Malakai nodded, though I could see a glimmer in his eye. "Thank you, Valentina. Knowing this will give my wife and me hope. Embry, I'm sorry we couldn't find your sister. We must both have faith in my son."

"I do," Embry replied. "The spirits spoke to me before he disappeared. They told me this was the only way."

"What?" I gasped. The moment he'd grunted in pain came flashing back. "That's why I felt your shock."

"Believe me, I want to do everything in my power to find both my sister and Daku, but Malakai is correct. As difficult as this is, we need to have faith that Daku will find her and bring them both home."

I could see right through his brave face. This news killed him. Wrapping both arms around his waist, I spoke privately through our link. *We'll find her. We'll find them both.*

I know, sweetheart. I know.

∞ ∞ ∞

EMBRY AND I LAY TOGETHER in our suite, windows open to the warm air. After staying up all night, I should have been exhausted. Instead, I found myself unable to sleep.

"You need your rest, sweetheart."

"I know."

"Yet you are still awake."

I rolled to face him, placing a palm against his bare chest. I didn't think I'd ever get used to the sight of Embry in the nude. "There's so much to think about. To decide."

"Perhaps I can help. What can we decide now that would help you sleep?"

"Where should we go from here?"

"We can go anywhere in the world."

"Embry..."

"What are our options?"

"Back to Wisconsin. Back to California, or New Mexico. Or...we could stay here."

He cupped my cheek. "Is that what you want? To stay here?"

"Here, or New Zealand. Reya and Tristan offered us a place to stay. I could train with her and Damien, and we could wait for Daku to come back with Rika."

"That could be years."

"So? I just have a feeling this is the right place for us to be, right now."

"Okay."

"Okay?"

"Yes. We can stay here, or with Reya and Tristan. You will expand your gift and we will wait for my sister's return."

"Wow. I feel better, having made the decision, but it's kind of a huge decision."

"We can visit your family whenever you wish. Or perhaps they would come here."

"You're right. I know you are, but it's still huge." I waited, tapping a nail against his muscle. "I also want to be converted."

Everything in him stilled. "Are you certain?"

"Of course. I wouldn't say so if I wasn't sure."

"Then that is what we will do. Anything else?"

"No, I think that's it."

Embry smiled. "I have one thing. Marry me, Valentina."

"Excuse me?"

"I think you heard me just fine."

"But—we—but..."

"You love me, yes?" I nodded. "And I love you. We are mates. I want to marry you in front of your family. Show them that I will take care of you, see to your health and happiness for all time."

"I—how can I say no to that?"

"There is no way. Just say yes."

He waited. I stared. Oh, what the hell. "Yes."

Dear Reader,

Thank you for reading *Vows at Dusk* and *After Dusk*!

I hope you enjoyed this reunion and that you will join us in Ireland as the next group attempts to infiltrate Murias in the otherworld. Meet Nadia as she navigates the world of the supernatural (and manages to put Jared in his place).

As always, you can keep up-to-date by following me on Facebook, Instagram, or TikTok @AnaBanNovels or by going to the website, www.anabannovels.com

Happy reading!

Always,

Ana

Other books by Ana Ban

www.anabannovels.com

The Parker Grey Series

Young Adult/Crime Novels recommended for ages 13+

Abstraction; A Parker Grey Novel (Book 1)

Backfire; A Parker Grey Novel (Book 2)

Coercion; A Parker Grey Novel (Book 3)

Deception; A Parker Grey Novel (Book 4)

Dubious Endeavors; A Parker Grey Novella (Book 5)

Exposed; A Parker Grey Novel (Book 6)

Firestarter; A Parker Grey Novel (Book 7)

The Gifted Series

Fantasy Romance Novels recommended for ages 18+

Allure of Home: Book 1 of The Gifted Series

Immaculate: Book 2 of The Gifted Series

Night Shift: Book 3 of The Gifted Series

Stow Away: Book 4 of The Gifted Series

Reservation: Book 5 of The Gifted Series

Shadowed Soul: Book 6 of The Gifted Series

Vows at Dusk: Book 7 of The Gifted Series (with bonus novella, *After Dusk*)

Dark Omens: Book 8 of The Gifted Series

By the Light of the Moon: Book 9 of The Gifted Series

Seeking Redemption: Book 10 of The Gifted Series

Shelter of Smoke: Book 11 of The Gifted Series

Tangled Threads: Book 12 of The Gifted Series

Beyond the Veil: Book 13 of The Gifted Series

Clash at Midnight: Book 14 of The Gifted Series (with bonus novella, *After Midnight*)

Legacy: Book 15 of The Gifted Series

Catching Shadows

Crime/Police Procedural Novel recommended for ages 18+

The Strangers Saga

Murder Mystery Romance Novels recommended for ages 18+

Baton Rouge: Book One

Baton Rouge: Book Two

Baton Rouge: Book Three

Baton Rouge: Book Four

Baton Rouge: Book Five